T 19529

DATE DUE

INNOVATIVE MINDS

RACHEL CARSON
PROTECTING OUR ENVIRONMENT

Barbara Ravage

RSVP
RAINTREE
STECK-VAUGHN
PUBLISHERS
The Steck-Vaughn Company

Austin, Texas

Copyright Permissions, Steck-Vaughn Company, P.O. Box 26015, Austin, TX 78755.

Published by Raintree Steck-Vaughn Publishers, an imprint of Steck-Vaughn Company.

Series created by Blackbirch Graphics
Series Editor: Tanya Lee Stone
Editor: Lisa Clyde Nielsen
Associate Editor: Elizabeth M. Taylor
Production/Design Editor: Calico Harington

Raintree Steck-Vaughn Staff
Editors: Shirley Shalit, Kathy DeVico
Project Manager: Lyda Guz

Library of Congress Cataloging-in-Publication Data

Ravage, Barbara.
   Rachel Carson: Protecting Our Environment / Barbara Ravage.
      p.   cm. — (Innovative minds)
   Includes bibliographical references (p.   ) and index.
   Summary: A biography of the American conservationist, biologist, and author.
   ISBN 0-8172-4406-9
   1. Carson, Rachel, 1907–1964—Juvenile literature. 2. Conservationists—United States—Biography—Juvenile literature. 3. Women conservationists—United States—Biography—Juvenile literature. 4. Science writers—United States—Biography—Juvenile literature. [1. Carson, Rachel, 1907–1964. 2. Conservationists. 3. Biologists. 4. Women—Biography] I. Title. II. Series.
QH31.C33R38   1997
574'.092—dc20
[B]
                                                           96-20313
                                                              CIP
                                                               AC

Printed in the United States of America
1 2 3 4 5 6 7 8 9 0   LB   00 99 98 97 96

TABLE OF CONTENTS

Rachel Carson was a scientist and writer who, through her books, shared her love of nature with millions of people.

A Childhood Close to Nature

When we think of important scientists, we usually picture them in laboratories, bent over microscopes, engaged in complex experiments. We remember them for their great discoveries.

For Rachel Carson, however, the Earth was her laboratory. Instead of a white lab coat, she wore sneakers, shorts or a bathing suit, and a brimmed hat to keep the sunlight off her pale face. She could most often be found hip-deep in saltwater or working late into the night at her typewriter.

Her great discovery concerned the web of life that encompasses all humankind, the plant and animal kingdoms, the sea and shoreline, and the air that nourishes—or poisons—all who live on the Earth. Her words were her lasting gift to the planet, and to us.

Rachel Carson broke barriers everywhere she went. At a time when women were not encouraged to be anything but wives and mothers, she attended college, went on to attend graduate school, and had a full professional life. At a time when few women pursued scientific careers, she became a highly regarded scientist. And at a time when few scientists were writers, Carson wrote books that would be read by millions of people.

In four groundbreaking books, Carson brought her scientific understanding to interested people everywhere throughout the world. But it was her fifth book, *Silent Spring*, that changed our world. In it, she sounded a warning that has altered the way the public, government, and industry behave.

Without intending to be, Carson became one of the founders of the environmental movement. Because she so strongly revered all living things, she was one of the greatest friends of the Earth.

A Different World

Rachel Carson was born on May 27, 1907. The world then was very different from the one in which we live today. The United States had not yet experienced the two tragic international conflicts we now call the world wars. Much of the country was still made up of small towns and rural areas, though the cities born of the Industrial Revolution were growing. There clearly were many advantages of industrial growth, but its disadvantages were just beginning to emerge when Carson was born. As a people, Americans were excited by the idea of new technology and had little notion that the price of "progress" was often pollution and destruction of the natural environment.

During her lifetime, Rachel Carson saw many changes, both good and bad, in the United States and the rest of the world. She fought against the worst of those changes and, in no small measure, was responsible for bringing about some of the best of them. To understand how she did that, we must go back to the town of Springdale, Pennsylvania, in the early years of the twentieth century.

The Carsons of Springdale

Springdale was a small town in Pennsylvania's Allegheny River Valley. Just 11 miles from the industrial center of Pittsburgh, it was surrounded by land that showed the scars of the enormous coal and steel industries that had made Pittsburgh famous.

The Carson family lived on a modest 65-acre farm. Their house was perched on a hill overlooking the town. Although they could hear the distant clatter of freight trains carrying coal to the blast furnaces and bringing iron and steel to a nation on the move, their home was encircled by woods, meadows, and orchards.

Robert Warden Carson and Maria McLean had met in the early 1890s through their common interest in music. Maria had been born in 1869 in Cleveland, Ohio, the daughter of a Presbyterian minister. The McLeans later settled in rural Pennsylvania. When the Reverend McLean died, Maria, then 11 years old, moved with her mother and sister to the small town of Washington, Pennsylvania. Robert lived in the city of Pittsburgh. He met Maria while visiting Washington

Maria Carson taught her children—Marian, Rachel, and Robert—to love nature and books.

as a member of a traveling church singing group. When they were married in 1894, Maria gave up her job as a teacher and turned her considerable energies toward raising a family.

The Carsons' first child, Marian, was born in 1897, followed two years later by Robert, Jr. The next year, the family bought a house and some land in Springdale.

Their home was a modest two-story dwelling with four rooms. It had neither electricity nor indoor plumbing—not uncommon in those days. Although the Carsons had an apple orchard and kept a few animals—a cow, some pigs, chickens, rabbits, and a horse to pull their carriage—Robert was not a farmer, nor did he plan to be. Instead, it was his intention to divide the 65 acres into smaller lots of land. He hoped to sell them to the growing numbers of workers who were moving to the towns around Pittsburgh as industries expanded into the countryside. But that plan, like so many others he had, did not work out.

Robert Carson was a soft-spoken man. He was a good man, but he did not have much of a head for business.

Supporting his family was always a struggle. The Carsons were not poor, but money was always tight. Robert worked part-time for the local electric company and also sold insurance. Maria helped as much as she could by giving piano lessons to local children.

Maria was a reserved and gentle person. She had an inner strength and determination. These qualities served both her and her family well. She was a lover of books and of nature—gifts she passed along to her children. She was also fiercely protective, however, and may have sheltered her children more than was necessary.

By the time Rachel Louise was born in 1907, Marian was ten and Robert, Jr., was eight. Because her brother and sister

As a child, Rachel often read to her favorite pet, Candy.

were already in school, Rachel spent her days with her mother or, more often, alone. Yet, although Rachel would later describe her childhood as solitary, she never considered it lonely. The hours when Robert and Marian were at school were filled with chores around the small farm and walks in the woods, first with her mother and, later, alone. It was there that she learned to identify birds by their songs and to recognize the trees and other plants that grew around her.

Rachel was an animal lover, too. Not only did she help care for the few farm animals the family owned, but she also always had at least one dog or cat, often more. A dog named Candy was a favorite childhood companion. Later she

Rachel had a love for nature at a very young age. As a girl, she learned about the birds and plants near her home.

would often speak of how helpful her cats were keeping her company during the hours that she spent writing her books.

In the evenings, Rachel eagerly absorbed everything her brother and sister shared with her of their lessons. After dinner, the family would sit by the fire while Maria read aloud. Maria would often play the piano while the others gathered around to sing. Despite the large age differences among them, the Carson children were very good friends in a closely knit family.

When Rachel was six years old, she entered Springdale Grammar School, eagerly following in her older siblings' footsteps. She was an excellent student, but rather shy. Although her teachers recognized her intelligence and curiosity, she did not make friends easily. Part of that may have had to do with how often she was absent from school. She had had scarlet fever as a young child, which had left her rather frail. Not only was she frequently sick with colds and other minor ailments, but her mother worried about her catching whatever was "going around." Maria often kept Rachel home when other children in her class were sick, or when the winter weather was severe. Rachel kept up with her lessons at home, helped by her mother's experience as a teacher and the love of learning they shared.

A Young Writer

Rachel's literary ambitions emerged when she was still very young. She loved to make up stories, and she simply assumed she would be a writer when she grew up. When she was ten years old, Rachel got some support for that goal and even earned her first money for her work.

She was in fourth grade, and big changes had taken place for her family as well as the rest of the world. War had broken out in Europe, and the United States joined in the fight against Germany and its allies. In 1917, Robert, Jr., enlisted in the U.S. Army Air Service. Although the family was proud of him, they also worried about his safety and waited anxiously for his letters to reach home. Those letters, filled with tales of bravery, captured Rachel's imagination.

A very popular magazine for children at the time, *St. Nicholas*, had invited its readers to contribute stories and poems to the St. Nicholas League. The best of them would be published, with the young authors receiving prize badges and cash payment. In 1917, Rachel sent in a story that she had written, entitled "A Battle in the Clouds." The story was about an air battle between a Canadian aviator and his German foes. It was inspired by Robert's letters and gave an extraordinarily vivid account of events that most young people could not even imagine. Much to Rachel's delight, the magazine published it in the September 1918 issue. She received $10 and the magazine's Silver Badge.

Within a year, two more of her stories—continuing her wartime theme—were published in *St. Nicholas*. They were "A Famous Sea Fight," which was set during the Spanish-American War of 1898, and "A Message to the Front," a World War I tale that won a Gold Badge. Rachel Carson was on her way to realizing her dream of being a professional writer.

Rachel's writing sprang directly from her love of reading, and she was an avid reader all her life. The stories she enjoyed the most as a child and young adult were about nature and its creatures.

She probably began her reading with Beatrix Potter's tales of Peter Rabbit and his friends. Later, she devoured the

Robert's letters home stimulated Rachel's imagination,
giving her ideas for war-themed stories. Here, Rachel,
Robert in his uniform, and Marian pose for the camera.

stories of Ernest Thompson Seton, who wrote many nature books for young people, including *Wild Animals I Have Known*. One of her favorite authors had a strong influence on her own writing. He was Henry Williamson, an Englishman who wrote *Tarka the Otter* and *Salar the Salmon*, two books that show readers a world of nature through the eyes of a wild creature.

In addition to a general love of nature, Rachel loved anything that was written about the sea. The poet John Masefield and novelists Joseph Conrad and Herman Melville described worlds that she had never seen in landlocked Springdale. It was almost as though the sea were beckoning her from afar, whispering that her future lay at the shore and upon the tides.

High School and Beyond

Rachel entered Springdale High School in 1921. At the time, students usually left school after two years, the boys going on to jobs, the girls to marry and raise families. Both Marian and Robert, Jr., had followed that course, Marian having married in 1917 and Robert, Jr., having moved to Pittsburgh in 1919 to work as an electrician after his discharge from the army at the end of the war. But Rachel, and her mother, knew that the youngest Carson was meant to continue her studies, even if providing for this would mean a financial struggle for the family.

Rachel took two more years of high school at Parnassus High, located 2 miles by streetcar from her home. She graduated from Parnassus in 1925, earning high honors and a small scholarship to Pennsylvania College for Women in Pittsburgh.

In college, Rachel (second from right in back row) was a member of the field-hockey team.

Going away to college was a big change for Rachel. She left her family and the small town of Springdale for a learning community of 300 young women in the big city. Her mother's frequent weekend visits kept her from feeling too lonely. Also, while she was still plagued by shyness, she did become involved in campus activities. She played basketball and field hockey, and worked on the student newspaper and the literary magazine. However, her greatest enthusiasm was for her studies, and she felt most at home among books and the teachers who recognized her special brilliance.

One of these teachers was Professor Grace Croff. Croff was pleased to have Rachel as an English major because, even at this early age, her writing talent shone brightly.

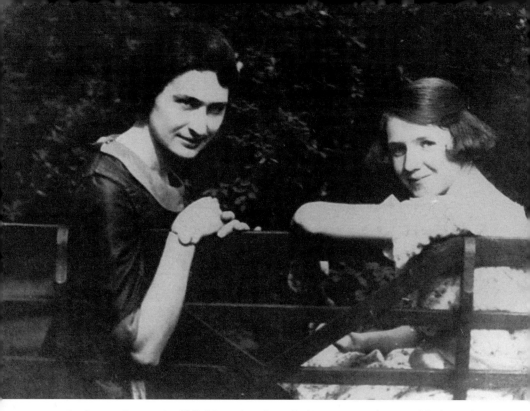

Professor Grace Croff (left) realized Rachel's writing talent and believed that her student would achieve success as a teacher or writer.

Croff expected that Rachel would distinguish herself as a teacher or even a writer. She was to prove an important influence in Rachel's life.

CARSON DISCOVERS SCIENCE

Rachel Carson had thought she would become a writer of poetry and fiction. To the surprise of everyone, Rachel included, a dramatic change took place in her second year at college. All students were required to take a science course even if they were not majoring in science. Carson chose biology, and a whole new world opened up to her.

Her guide in that world was a young instructor named Mary Scott Skinker. She was one of those truly outstanding teachers who can make a subject fascinating and inspire her students to explore directions they otherwise might not have considered. Carson found the study of biology exciting and challenging, and she loved the field trips her teacher led—advanced versions of her childhood nature walks with her mother.

In her later work, Carson always communicated a sense of wonder at nature. She thought it was especially important that children be introduced to the natural world at an early age, as she had been, when their senses were open to all that lay around them. She even wrote a magazine article, which was later turned into a book, advising parents to "Help Your Child to Wonder." Carson's mother had done just that and now, as a young woman in college, she took the next step, with Skinker as her guide.

Learning about the outdoor world led Rachel Carson to an even greater appreciation of nature. Before long, she was considering abandoning her plans to be a writer and studying science instead. It was a big decision. It would mean giving up a long-held dream and disappointing people like Professor Croff, who had such high hopes for her literary talents. But more than that, it was terribly impractical in that era. Women could be writers, and they certainly could be teachers, especially in subjects like literature, but science was considered a world for men. If Carson chose science, she would be wading into uncharted waters.

Carson had rare inner strength and courage, however. She did not shrink from challenges, and she never considered a road to be blocked just because no one else had traveled on it. Deciding to switch her major to zoology, the study of the animal kingdom, was a big step for her. Many people she respected told her that there was no real place for a woman in the world of science. Nonetheless, science was what she cared about, and if she was to be a pioneer, she had her vast energy and intellectual curiosity to help her.

In Skinker, Carson also had a mentor—an older, more experienced person to guide and advise her. This sort of guidance would come to Carson often during her life as she found other mentors at important turning points in her career. And not only was she lucky enough to find them, but she was wise enough to make the most of their advice and direction.

Carson had Skinker as her teacher for only one more year, though they remained friends until the older woman died in 1950. In 1928, Skinker left her teaching post at the college to study for a doctorate (an advanced degree) at Johns Hopkins University in Baltimore, Maryland. That prestigious institution, long known for the excellence of its science and medical departments, had few women students. Skinker was one of them, and she wrote Carson excited letters about her work, urging her most promising student to consider coming to Johns Hopkins to continue working toward a career in science.

Once she decided to switch her field of study, Carson faced a daunting set of challenges. Beginning in her junior year, she took a double load of science courses to make up for the first two years in which she had concentrated on literary studies. She also had to earn extra money, to help with her college tuition. Her $100 scholarship hardly made a dent in her tuition and living costs, so she tutored students in Springdale during the summer between her junior and senior years and earned about $75 more. Her parents contributed as much as they could, even selling their antique china to help pay the bills. But money had never been plentiful in the Carson household, and Rachel graduated from college in 1929 with a mountain of debts to go along with her *magna cum laude* (high honors) degree.

GRADUATION AND BEYOND

Carson took the hand that Skinker had extended from Johns Hopkins and applied for the master's (a degree after college level) program at Hopkins in marine zoology. With Skinker's recommendation and that of other faculty and the administration at Pennsylvania College for Women, Carson was accepted with a full scholarship for tuition. She would begin in the fall of 1929. But first, she was given the opportunity to have an exceptional experience.

Through Skinker's help, Carson won a six-week summer internship—a temporary job for promising young people—at the Marine Biological Laboratory (MBL) in Woods Hole, on Cape Cod in Massachusetts. In the summer of 1929, she set off on the journey to Massachusetts. It was farther than she had ever been from home and family, but she felt she was going to meet her destiny—the sea.

A FIRST GLIMPSE OF THE SEA

Carson traveled by train to New York City and from there by boat to the coastal city of New Bedford, Massachusetts, and finally to nearby Woods Hole. It was on that journey that she saw the ocean for the first time, though she had loved the idea and images of its vastness from childhood.

Once at MBL, she joined a community of scientists unlike anything she had ever imagined. Although she was a "beginning investigator," and one of very few women there, Carson had access to the laboratories and research facilities. She could also use MBL's library, to which she would return

What's Happening in Woods Hole?

Woods Hole, Massachusetts, is a charming old port town at the southwestern tip of Cape Cod. Its location makes it an ideal place to study marine life. Just offshore, the cold northern currents from Canada meet the warm southern waters of the Gulf Stream. Thus, an extraordinary variety of marine life can be found in Woods Hole's backyard.

Every morning, a Marine Biological Laboratory boat named the *Gemma* sets out to gather specimens of marine life. Researchers put in their "orders" for specimens as though from a restaurant menu, and get what they've asked for with the morning tide. In addition, MBL supplies more than 100,000 examples of 200 species of marine life to scientists around the world.

The MBL, where Rachel Carson spent six exciting weeks in 1929, is an independent research center that was founded in 1888. Despite its name, the laboratory is involved in much more than the study of ocean life. It is devoted to research and education in such diverse areas as cell and developmental biology, ecology, neurobiology, sensory physiology, microbiology, marine biomedicine, and molecular evolution.

The creatures of the sea are particularly well suited for scientific experiments and observations that relate to higher species, including human beings. This is because their body systems are simple versions of those found in more complex organisms.

The squid, for example, has a single, very large axon—the part of a nerve cell that carries messages to other nerve cells. Humans, in comparison, have millions of axons, and they are too tiny to be seen by the naked eye. But by studying the squid, researchers can learn important things about how our own nerves work. Another marine specimen, the horseshoe crab, was the subject of a test developed at MBL that can detect blood poisoning in humans. It is now used throughout the world.

Sea urchins, dogfish (a small member of the shark family), clams, starfish, toadfish, sea slugs, and sponges are all helping MBL researchers to learn more about more than a dozen diseases, ranging from AIDS and birth defects to learning disorders and cancer.

In addition to MBL, Woods Hole is the home of the National Marine Fisheries Service, the Woods Hole Oceanographic Institution, and the United States Geological Survey. It is truly an international center for natural science research, attracting scientists and students from all over the world.

Parts of many of these organizations are open to the general public. Visitors can take tours of MBL, the Exhibit Center at the Oceanographic Institution, and the National Marine Fisheries Service Aquarium. Oceanquest offers "discovery voyages" aboard a fully equipped research vessel.

For more information, you can call MBL at 508-289-7623; the Oceanographic Institution Exhibit Center at 508-457-2100; the Aquarium at 508-548-7684; and Oceanquest at 800-37-OCEAN.

An aerial view of the Marine Biological Laboratories shows the main buildings of the research center.

Carson's summer internship at Woods Hole allowed her access to all of MBL's facilities. Here, she sits on the deck of a research boat.

years later when writing about the sea and shore. But best of all, she was able to share in the spirit of discovery with the scientists who gathered there. Happily, Mary Frye, a close friend from college and a fellow science major, was also there that summer, and the two of them shared a room in the quaint little fishing village of Woods Hole. Carson found new friends among the tightly knit community of MBL as well.

Carson spent her days in the laboratory, working side by side with researchers far older and more experienced than she. Her project was related to the nervous system of turtles, and the paper she wrote about it was judged good enough to submit to a scientific journal. During her free time, she often joined the friendly group of scientists for picnics and beach walks and other social gatherings. For the first time in her life, the shy and solitary young woman was among people who shared her interests, and in an extraordinary place to explore it all. It is almost as though she had found her true home by traveling hundreds of miles away from Springdale.

OUT

IN THE

WORLD

Fired up with enthusiasm after her Woods Hole summer, Carson moved to Baltimore and prepared to immerse herself in her studies at Johns Hopkins. But first she paid a visit to Elmer Higgins, a man who would play an important part in her life. Although their first meeting was anything but encouraging, in Higgins she was to find another mentor.

Back in 1929, the federal government agency most closely concerned with marine biology was the Bureau of Fisheries, then under the direction of the U.S. Department of Commerce. It was headquartered in Washington, D.C., about an hour south of Baltimore. Higgins was the head of the bureau's Division of Scientific Inquiry. He had a reputation for being generous with his time and advice, particularly

Carson registered at Hopkins with plans to get her master's degree.

when approached by young scientists. Although all those young scientists had always been men, Carson worked up the nerve to call on him.

What she wanted to know was what kind of jobs might be available to someone holding a master's degree in marine zoology from Johns Hopkins and what courses she should take to prepare herself for such a job. Carson's approach was typically forward-thinking. It was rare then, and is rare still, to find a 22-year-old with the courage and foresight to ask those questions of a stranger before heading off in search of a dream.

In the kindest way possible, Higgins told Carson that the best she could hope for was a teaching position. Women simply were not hired by private industry, he said. Research institutions and museums, whether they were private or public, would not consider a woman either. And, as for the government, it was not hiring anybody at the time. When it did, he added, female employees were invariably either secretaries or file clerks. In his opinion, there was little or no chance for advancement for women.

It may have been a difficult message for Carson to hear, but it probably did not surprise her. Professional opportunities

Was Rachel Carson a Feminist?

Rachel Carson encountered, and overcame, gender (sex) discrimination as a woman in the "man's world" of science. She is a powerful role model for young women working in that and other professions. But can we think of her as a feminist—someone who actively works for women's political, economic, and social equality with men?

Carson never took part in any organized movement for women's rights. She was a schoolgirl when women were fighting for the vote, and she had died by the time "Feminism" and "Women's Liberation" were cries heard across the land. The fight that Carson chose to pursue was a different one—she fought to protect the natural environment. It is, perhaps, unlikely that she would have answered the call of the women's movement even had she been around to hear it, as she was focused on things that piqued her curiosity—whether they were done by men or by women.

When Rachel Carson first became famous, with her best-selling book *The Sea Around Us*, many of her fans and others familiar with her work assumed that she was a person of imposing physical as well as intellectual stature. (One reader of the time simply assumed that she was a man, because of her great knowledge of the subject.) In fact, she was reserved, soft-spoken, and characterized by people who knew her as a refined and even "ladylike" individual. At five feet, four inches, she was not a tall person, and with her fair skin and delicate features, many people did not perceive her as a very powerful one. But the inner strength and courage she exhibited all her life made her truly heroic.

It is striking to us today, when reading Rachel Carson's work, how often she uses the pronoun *he* and the words *man* and *mankind*. Many writers today, whether they are men or women, try not to use such "gender-specific" references. But it is important not to make too much of this aspect of her writing. It was the style of the times. In those days, few writers thought about how the use of such words could make people feel excluded.

for women were extremely narrow in the first half of the twentieth century. It had been less than a decade since women had even been granted the right to vote. It would be another four decades before the feminist movement would bring about sweeping changes for women in their professional and personal lives. Carson was facing a hard reality, but she did not back down from the challenge.

Higgins liked Carson, and he admired her attitude. He wished her good luck, inviting her to stop by again after she finished her studies at Hopkins.

A Dark Time

Soon after she began studying at Johns Hopkins, Carson's personal battle was dwarfed by the collapse of the American economy and the worldwide economic depression that followed. Its impact on her family was felt almost immediately.

There was no chance of supporting the Carson family on the income from the Springdale farm, and the prospect of selling the land was now an impossibility. Scores of people were losing their land, and no one had the money—or the confidence in the economy—to buy property. Carson convinced her parents that it would be best to give up the farm and move with her into a small house near Baltimore. Her brother, Robert, was one of the 15 million Americans who lost their jobs, and he moved in for a while as well. He did odd jobs, most of them electrical, including repairing radios. But the pay he received was meager. Her father also found small jobs from time to time, but as a man in his 60s at a time when younger and more vigorous men were without work, his chances were slim.

Johns Hopkins and Beyond

Throughout this difficult time, Carson began the demanding work required for a master's degree, but she also needed to earn some money. This she did by working as a lab assistant—washing test tubes, setting up equipment, and keeping track of supplies. She also taught a lower-level course in zoology at Hopkins during summer school. Later, she took a part-time teaching job at the University of Maryland, in College Park, a one-hour bus trip from home. Combined with nearly 40 hours of classes per week each semester and all the studying and lab time required, she was very busy indeed.

In what little spare time she had, Carson wrote poetry. She tried for a while to get her poems published, but the rejection slips piled up. She continued to write, though, because

This photo of Johns Hopkins was taken in 1931, around the time that Carson was working there.

THE GREAT DEPRESSION

On October 29, 1929, the New York stock market crashed, bringing down the entire American economy with it. Throughout the country, banks and businesses failed. Millions of people lost their savings, their jobs, and their homes. Farmers were particularly hard hit. At one point, more than a third of the workforce were without jobs, and the average income of Americans as a whole had dropped by 50 percent.

This "Great Depression" was a time of despair. Millions were homeless, living in cars or in "tent cities." Food was expensive and scarce. Many people died as a result of lack of food, clothing, and shelter. Schools closed because there was no money to pay teachers or even to keep the buildings open. Marriage and birth rates declined. And because the United States was the world's leading economic power, the Depression spread to Europe as well.

When Franklin Delano Roosevelt became President in 1933, he began a recovery program called the New Deal. He established the National Recovery Administration (NRA) and a host of government agencies and policies, including the National Industrial Recovery Act (NIRA), the Agricultural Adjustment Administration (AAA), the Public Works Administration (PWA), the Work Projects Administration (WPA), and the Civilian Conservation Corps (CCC). There was even a National Youth Administration (NYA). With all the initials that stood for those administrations, some people joked that Roosevelt was giving the country "alphabet soup."

Laws were passed to ensure that bank failures would not rob people of their life's savings. Job programs were created to rebuild the

it was a private pleasure and provided a refuge from her crushing responsibilities at home and in school.

Her main project at school involved the catfish and an odd little organ, a sort of temporary kidney, that develops during the catfish's embryonic state (an early stage of development).

country at the same time as they provided employment for millions. Loans were made to homeowners. The Social Security system was established to provide workers with income after they retired, and aid was provided for farmers to ensure a ready food supply.

It took a long time, however, for public confidence to be restored and for the country to regain its economic health. It was not until the 1940s that the United States really got back on its feet, and then it was because industrial production began to boom due to preparation for World War II. It is ironic that wars, which cause so much destruction, are often the best medicine for an ailing economy.

People stand in line for free bread and milk during the Great Depression.

After about 11 days, the temporary kidney is replaced by a permanent one in a different part of the fish's body. The report Carson wrote—called a "thesis," a paper needed to receive a master's degree—had the tongue-twisting title "The Development of the Pronephros During the Embryonic

Carson examined embryonic catfish eggs, such
as these, as a part of her thesis research.

and Early Larval Life of the Catfish (*Inctalurus punctatus*)." It
was not an earthshaking study—few master's degree
projects are—but in the course of it, Carson learned a tremendous amount about scientific research, methodology, and
writing. She also learned how to make scientific drawings
and photomicrographs (photographs made of an image seen
through a microscope) of specimens. This disciplined practice would stay with her and contribute to the solidness of all
her future work. She had always had a way with words; now
her graduate work was adding to her skills.

Carson received her master's degree in 1932, when she
was 25. Although she had always insisted that she did not
want to be a teacher, her Johns Hopkins and University of
Maryland positions were all that was available, and she felt

lucky to have them. However, her income from these two jobs was not enough to pay the bills, and her University of Maryland job ended in December 1933. It was then that she realized that she could combine her two loves, science and writing, to earn some extra money.

A Writer and a Scientist

Ever since her second year of college, when Carson faced the dilemma of choosing between majoring in science or English, she had believed that she had to commit herself to one world or the other. Now she realized that she could combine her talents and interests. Her fascination with the marine world, and her growing knowledge about it, had given her something to write about.

The first money that Carson earned writing about the underwater world was from articles about fishing that she wrote for *The Baltimore Sunday Sun* newspaper, beginning in 1936. One of her articles described the migration of eels from the Chesapeake Bay to the Sargasso Sea, a salty and seaweed-clotted area in the mid-Atlantic Ocean. This area is as large as the United States and stretches as far north as the Chesapeake Bay and as far south as the island of Haiti. Carson would later use parts of that article in her first book, *Under the Sea-Wind*. At about $10 per article, the money did not amount to much, but it helped a bit, and it gave her some confidence.

That confidence was sorely needed. In 1935, her father had died suddenly, probably of a heart attack. Now Rachel was the head of a grieving family, and her responsibilities doubled. Her brother, who had by then moved away, was unable to help out financially. And her sister, Marian, was a busy single mother with two young children. Marian was also in poor health and was often hospitalized.

Carson remembered Elmer Higgins and the door that he had left open to her when she had visited him as a young college graduate. She called on him again, and the timing, it turned out, was perfect.

Higgins had a problem. The Bureau of Fisheries was supposed to be producing a series of 52 weekly radio programs, entitled "Romance under the Waters." The programs, which the bureau staff jokingly referred to as "Seven-Minute Fish

In her "Fish Tales," Carson provided solid information on undersea life in an entertaining way and was given a chance to work as a writer.

Tales," were meant to give average radio listeners an idea about marine life. The scripts had to be brief, informative, entertaining, and easy to understand. The problem was, no one on Higgins's staff had both the necessary scientific knowledge and the ability to write clear and lively material for people who were not scientists. Enter Rachel Carson.

Higgins remembered the spirited young woman, and even though he knew nothing about her writing skills, he was willing to take a chance. Giving her a sample script as a model to follow, he assigned her to write three programs. He would pay a little less than $20 for each one. It was not an official government job, and there was no guarantee of more work when the series was finished, but it was work—*writing work*—and Rachel accepted it with enthusiasm.

Higgins's intuition paid off. Carson's first three "Fish Tales" were a great success. He now offered her a job as a part-time writer, at a salary of $1,000 a year. In the 1930s, in Depression-ravaged America, that was a respectable amount of money. More important, it was steady work related to Carson's interests. She continued to write articles occasionally for the *Sunday Sun* as well, supplementing her income and drawing on information available to her through the Bureau of Fisheries.

NEW RESPONSIBILITIES, NEW OPPORTUNITIES

Just when things were beginning to look brighter, the Carson family suffered another crushing blow: Marian died of pneumonia at the age of 40. Rachel and her mother took in Marian's two young daughters, Marjorie and Virginia, but the expanded family required a larger house and, of course, more money. The Carsons moved to Silver Spring, Maryland, a suburb that was nearer to Rachel's work in Washington, D.C. Rachel shared parenting responsibilities with her mother. But one of her nieces later said that Rachel was more like a fun older sister than a mother. She was also the sole financial supporter of the family.

It was a piece of good luck that a new job opened up at the Bureau of Fisheries for a junior aquatic biologist. Because it was a government job, applicants had to take a civil-service examination. The job would go to the person with the highest score. Carson was the only woman to take the exam, and her score was the highest. Beginning in August 1936, she was assigned to Higgins's office, at a permanent, full-time salary of $2,000 a year.

When she had first met her mentor seven years earlier, he had not been very encouraging about the hope for a job for anyone, let alone a woman. Now her mentor was her boss. Both Carson and Higgins highly valued the friendship and professional relationship that developed between them during this time.

After Carson finished the radio scripts, her next assignment was to turn the scripts into pamphlets. When people wrote to the Bureau of Fisheries asking for information about fish and fishing, they would be sent a pamphlet. If none existed, Carson would do research on the question and reply by letter. If enough people asked the same questions, Carson would write a new pamphlet on that topic. She was also asked to put together a larger publication that collected the "Fish Tales" pamphlets into one booklet, introduced by a general, introductory essay about the sea.

Carson worked long and hard on the introductory essay. Writing was a painstaking process for her. She first wrote a draft by hand, and then revised it again and again. She wanted her message to be clear, but her words had to sound right, too. Perhaps this was because she was also a poet, or because of her earlier experience writing radio scripts, which were meant to be *heard*, not read. Her mother often read the drafts out loud so that Rachel could catch anything that did not sound just right. Then it was back to work with pencil and paper. When she was satisfied, she or her mother typed the final draft.

Carson's essay, "Undersea," ended up being nearly 25 pages long, and it was extremely well written. Higgins admired her work, but thought it was much too literary for the Bureau of Fisheries. He asked her to try again, but added that the essay she had written deserved to be published.

He suggested that Carson send it to *The Atlantic Monthly*—a magazine that, despite its name, had nothing to do with the ocean. Instead, it was a literary journal famous for the excellence of the writing that appeared in it. In the past, *The Atlantic* had published the likes of Henry David Thoreau and Ralph Waldo Emerson.

Carson was hesitant, but finally she took her mentor's advice and sent the article to *The Atlantic*. The magazine accepted it, paying her $75 for "Undersea" and publishing it in the September 1937 issue. This first appearance in a national publication brought Carson's special way with words and her subject to the attention of a sophisticated and influential reading public—including two people who would play important roles in her growth as a writer.

CHAPTER THREE

SHE
FINDS HER
SUBJECT

In "Undersea," Carson introduced a world unknown to most people. Inventions such as SCUBA—a self-contained underwater breathing apparatus—had not yet been created, and most of the vast and deep oceans of the world were uncharted territory, even for scientists. Many people had never even seen the ocean. Those who visited or lived near it might know a thing or two about the tides or the fish and shellfish near the shore, but nothing of its greater depths—the creatures that lived there and the undersea mountains and valleys that dwarf anything seen on land.

A New Way of Thinking and Writing about Nature

As a writer, Carson was both poet and scientist. As always, she brought to her work a sense of wonder about the natural world. Here are some lines from her essay "Undersea":

> *Thus we see the parts of the plan fall into place: the water receiving from earth and air the simple materials, storing them up until the gathering energy of the spring sun wakens the sleeping plants to a burst of dynamic activity, hungry swarms of planktonic animals growing and multiplying upon the abundant plants, and themselves falling prey to the shoals of fish; all, in the end, to be redissolved into their component substances when the inexorable laws of the sea demand it....Against this cosmic background the life span of a particular plant or animal appears, not as a drama complete in itself, but only as a brief interlude in a panorama of endless change.*

Planktonic animals, such as these zooplankton, feed on plants, and, in turn, are fed upon by fish.

Carson wrote about the natural world in a new way. Rather than describing one or even many single organisms, she chose to write about the total environment, the ecosystem to which the living creatures belonged. Carson was writing from an *ecological* point of view, which was at the time a relatively new way of studying and thinking about living things. She was to approach all of her work from that point of view, even in the pamphlets that she wrote to educate American families about the seafood that ended up on their dinner tables. Indeed, Rachel Carson believed that it was very important to know everything about a fish before cooking and eating it.

RECOGNITION

Many people who read *The Atlantic Monthly* enjoyed Carson's essay and wrote words of praise to the magazine and to Carson herself. Two of the letters she received were especially important. The first came from a man named Quincy Howe, the editor-in-chief at the New York publishing company of Simon and Schuster. He asked whether she would consider writing a longer work, a book that told more about the sea in the same wonderful way she had done in her essay. He asked Carson to consider submitting the idea to his company.

The second letter came from Hendrik Willem van Loon, who had written a best-selling book entitled *The Story of Mankind*. Recognition from such a famous writer meant a lot to Carson, as did his explanation for his interest in her: He felt that she could tell him the things he wanted to know about the ocean.

What Is Ecology?

Ecology is the science of the interactions between living things and their environment. It encompasses the life cycles of animals and plants; climate and weather; air, water, and soil; natural land formations; and even cities and structures made by people. It looks at all the processes that influence the entire community of living things, also called an ecosystem.

The word *ecology* comes from the Greek word *oikos*, meaning "house." The term was invented by a German zoologist named Ernst Haeckel in 1866 to describe the study of how living things interact with one another in a shared habitat. The term was not widely used until the twentieth century, however, and did not come to the attention of the general public until the 1960s.

For scientists, ecology usually means the field study—as opposed to work in a laboratory—of biological processes. For the public, it emphasizes how humans affect the environment, with particular attention to air and water pollution through chemical and industrial contamination, waste disposal, and the loss of wilderness areas. Some people care mostly about the impact on human health and quality of life; others are also concerned about endangered species and the future of the planet Earth as a whole.

In 1939, van Loon invited Carson to visit him at home in Connecticut, and arranged for Howe to join them for dinner. That evening, the two men encouraged her to try writing a book and gave her valuable advice on how to go about it. She returned to Silver Spring fired up with the idea and set to work immediately on a book. It would be called *Under the Sea-Wind*. Carson was able to send Howe enough of the manuscript in 1939 to get a contract with his publishing company and an advance payment of $500 against future sales of the book from Simon and Schuster. But with all of her responsibilities, completing the book was going to prove to be a challenging task.

Work and More Work

At the same time that she was trying to write her first book, Carson was working full-time at the Bureau of Fisheries. Then, in 1940, Fisheries merged with the Bureau of Biological Survey to form the U.S. Fish and Wildlife Service. No longer a part of the Department of Commerce, it became—and still is—an agency of the Department of the Interior.

During the day, Carson answered queries and wrote informative pieces for the public and the fishing industry. In the evenings, life centered around her family; her mother and her nieces relied heavily on her. That left only the hours after everyone else had gone to bed for writing. Carson got into the habit of writing long into the night, with her Persian cats Kito and Buzzie keeping her company.

Carson loved doing research, especially if it meant being outdoors, but she found the process of writing agonizingly slow. She rarely managed more than two pages a night, and everything she wrote was revised many times over. This would be true throughout her life. No matter how successful her books were, writing was always difficult for her.

As before, her mother, Maria, was a great help, reading aloud and typing the final draft. When the book was finished, Rachel dedicated it simply "To my Mother." She sent the manuscript off to Simon and Schuster exactly on time to meet her deadline: December 31, 1940.

UNDER THE SEA-WIND

Carson's first book followed the approach that had won so much praise for "Undersea." It focused on living creatures in their environments. She chose three locales—the shore, the open sea, and the ocean floor—and, as main "characters," representative animals that lived in each. She called them by their scientific names, but wrote about them as individuals. Rynchops is a skimmer, a shore bird, that migrates to the North Carolina seacoast; Scomber, a mackerel, lives in the cold waters of the North Atlantic; and Anguilla, an eel, journeys from the rivers that empty into the Chesapeake Bay to the salty bottom of the Sargasso Sea.

Carson was influenced by the Henry Williamson books that she had read when she was younger, *Tarka the Otter* and *Salar the Salmon*. By writing from the point of view of wild animals, she sought to give readers a sense of the creatures' daily experience—where and how they lived, how and what they ate, what dangers they faced. In addition to the main characters, the book is "peopled" by birds, fish, and animals such as snowy owls, comb jellyfish and lemmings, big-eyed shrimp and tiny noctiluca, one-celled phosphorescent creatures that light up the sea, and many more. The narrative style of *Under the Sea-Wind* makes it a pleasure for readers of all ages.

The book was published in November 1941, when Carson was 34. It won good reviews and the praise of many people in the scientific community. One of its fans was Dr. William Beebe, a well-known marine biologist who would become another mentor to Carson. The book was included as a selection of the Scientific Book Club, and editions for the

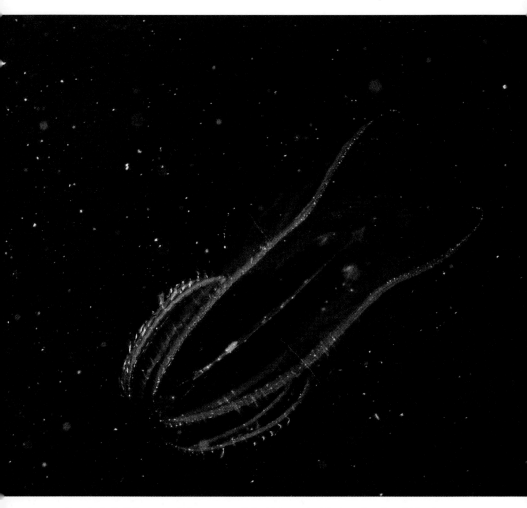

Comb jellyfish were "characters" in Carson's *Under the Sea-Wind*.

visually impaired, both in Braille and Talking Books, were also planned.

The book sold only about 5,000 copies, and Rachel earned less than $1,000 from the first edition. She told a friend that writing short pieces for magazines and newspapers was a more reliable way to earn money. It was a very discouraging outcome for more than three years of hard work.

War Breaks Out

If *Under the Sea-Wind* failed to be a big hit, it was mostly because Americans were distracted by more important events. Just over a month after the book was published, the Japanese attacked Pearl Harbor, and the United States entered World War II. People were not buying books about nature; they were worrying about their future and the future of the human race.

One of the beneficial outcomes of the war was the explosion of knowledge about the sea. Oceanography, the science of the earth's vast saltwater regions, suddenly was important from a military point of view. The war was being fought in both the Atlantic and Pacific Oceans. Submarines prowled the silent depths while battleships and troop carriers navigated on the surface. Knowledge about tides, currents, and underwater geography was essential. In fact, the D-Day invasion, which marked a turning point in the war, could not have been successfully planned without such information.

Carson was not directly involved in oceanographic research, but she had learned about it through her work and her contact with many other professionals. When it came time for her to write her next book, *The Sea Around Us*, she drew heavily on the advances in oceanography that had come about through the needs of a nation at war.

She also learned about the new chemical pesticide dichloro-diphenyl-trichloroethane (DDT), used by the military to protect soldiers from insect-borne diseases. She was concerned about the long-term effects of such chemicals—both on humans and on the environment. Years later, she would return to the subject in her most important book of all, *Silent Spring*.

Life with the Service

In her job at the Fish and Wildlife Service, Carson did find herself somewhat involved in the war effort (though she told a friend that she wished she could do something more valuable to help the country in wartime). Her assignment was to prepare a series of "Conservation Bulletins," 50-page booklets intended to encourage people to eat more fish at a time when other protein foods were scarce. Even though the idea was to introduce homemakers to the great variety of local fish and give practical tips on how to prepare them, Carson used it as an opportunity to tell people more. In her introduction, she explained that enjoyment of the food is enhanced by knowing "something of the creatures from which they are derived, how and where they live, how they are caught, their habits and migrations."

In her discussion of clams, for example, she began explaining that the clam that finds its way into our chowder begins life as one of millions of tiny swimming embryos only 1/300 of an inch long. If it survives temperature changes and the threat of being gobbled up by jellyfish and other predators, it loses its ability to swim after a few days. It develops a muscular digging appendage and descends to the sandy bottom. For a while, the tiny creature anchors itself to a piece of seaweed or a small rock or shell and begins to develop a shell of its own. The dangers to its survival during that period are crabs, small fish, and baby starfish. Finally, its shell thickened and its size increased to about one quarter of an inch, it burrows down into the relative safety of the ocean floor. Readers of these government publications got a real education along with their recipes!

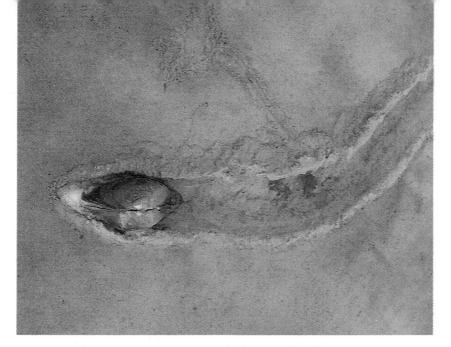

Carson took every opportunity to include scientific information in her writing for the general public, such as how a clam uses its muscular appendage to dig through the sand.

In 1942, the Fish and Wildlife Service was temporarily relocated to Chicago, Illinois. Office space was scarce in the nation's capital and was needed for workers essential to the war effort. So Carson and her family pulled up stakes and moved to the Midwest, though they were gone for less than a year. It was the sort of disruption that people had to get used to in wartime. Carson's enthusiasm for her job was waning, and the move to Chicago added to her growing thought that it was time to look for a more exciting job.

RESTLESS TIMES

Carson was becoming restless. She was in her mid-30s and wondered what she was doing with her life. She longed to do more creative writing, to have time to pursue the things she thought were important, and she needed to make more money to support her family. She tried for a while to find a different job. She wrote to the New York Zoological Society, *Reader's Digest,* and the National Audubon Society. She spread the word among her friends and mentors that she would consider making a change. But nothing came of these efforts to find something new.

Carson had not given up her dream of being a writer. She even told a friend that for her, an ideal existence would be to make a living from her writing alone. Still, she knew that the kind of "nature writing" that sold—brief articles about odd facts of the natural world—was not the kind she cared to do. She wanted to write things that would give people a deeper appreciation of nature.

On evenings and weekends, she wrote nature articles and submitted them to various magazines, but except for a piece about starlings in *Nature* magazine, she had little luck. Then, in 1944, she wrote about how bats "see" in the dark, using a sense she compared to radar, then a new military technology. "The Bat Knew It First" was published in *Collier's* magazine, and a condensed (shortened) version was printed in *Reader's Digest*. Although Carson knew it was not a great piece of writing, it earned her more than $500 and was even reprinted by the U.S. Navy, which considered it a wonderfully clear explanation of radar for the general public.

Despite her discontent with her job at the Fish and Wildlife Service, Carson was promoted to positions of increasingly greater authority and responsibility—from junior aquatic biologist to assistant aquatic biologist to associate aquatic biologist to aquatic biologist and finally, in 1945—as World War II was ending—to information specialist. In addition to writing, she also began editing the work of other writers.

Carson's good friend, Shirley Briggs,
accompanied her on bird-watching trips.

The people with whom Carson worked said that she was
a tough editor who demanded excellent work from others,
but she was also fair and a lot of fun. The door to her office
was always open, and she enjoyed lighthearted lunch breaks
with her coworkers, who called her Ray. Despite the dreary
wartime and the dull nature of writing recipe booklets,
Carson found time for humor. She joined her colleagues in
practical jokes, including a famous one, planned but never
pulled off, that involved writing a recipe for field mice in a
mushroom-and-wine sauce.

Her close friend during that period was Shirley Briggs,
who joined the Service in 1945 as an artist and writer. She
designed the publications. On days off, the two went on

Years after she wrote about refuges, Carson would be
honored by having a wildlife refuge named for her.

bird-watching treks with the local Audubon Society and
even managed field trips associated with their work.

By then, Carson was in charge of a series of booklets called
"Conservation in Action," each devoted to one of the national wildlife refuges. The refuges had been established by the
Department of the Interior to protect wild spaces and the
species that live there from the rising tide of development in
postwar America.

It was a time when towns and cities were growing, and a
vast network of superhighways was being built across the
land. As a result, many wilderness areas were being lost to

development. People were not giving enough thought to the consequences of development and the importance of conserving natural habitats. The Department of the Interior did recognize the problem and tried to take action by creating wildlife refuges and parklands, but it was often at odds with other government and business interests.

Carson wrote some of the conservation booklets and guided the writers of others. That gave her and Briggs an excuse to take some memorable trips: They watched migrating hawks in the Appalachian Mountains of Pennsylvania, explored the shoreline of Chincoteague off the coast of Maryland, and even scouted out the Florida Everglades.

Carson also enjoyed an active social life. It centered around the scientific and academic community that had gathered in Washington, D.C., during and after the war. There she found friends who shared her interest not only in nature, but also in literature and the arts. Shirley Briggs remembered it as a busy and happy time for both of them.

In 1949, Carson became chief editor of the Service. In addition to assigning, reviewing, and editing manuscripts, she wrote speeches for government officials. Her skills as an editor and manager were put to good use in what amounted to running a small publishing company with a staff of six.

SHE RETURNS TO THE SEA

Even before she took on the added responsibility of chief editor, Carson had begun a new project of her own. She was doing research for a book that she later said she had been working on all her life. It was a book about the sea itself, and it would include the latest knowledge gained by wartime

Carson loved the sea, and she shared
her sense of wonder with her readers.

oceanographic studies. This book would communicate
Carson's deep fascination with—and emotional attachment
to—the undersea world and, as always, her sense of wonder.
Her working title was "Return to the Sea"; at various times,
the project was called "Mother Sea," "The Empire of the
Sea," and even, as a joke, "Out of My Depth." The whole
world now knows it as *The Sea Around Us.*

Carson's research for the book was exhaustive. She read more than 1,000 books, articles, and technical papers. She consulted librarians, oceanographers, explorers, and experts in many fields from universities, museums, and research institutions the world over. Among the hundreds of people she corresponded with were her mentor William Beebe, and the explorer and adventurer Thor Heyerdahl, whose Pacific voyage aboard a raft is recorded in his world-famous book *Kon-Tiki*.

By the summer of 1948, Carson had worked out a plan for the book and outlined the chapters. But she still had much research and the grinding work of actual writing ahead of her. Rather than just plunge into the work, she decided to follow the advice of friends who knew the publishing business. Before spending more time and money on the project, she decided to get a contract from a publisher. In order to do that, she would need to find a literary agent to handle the business and practical details.

Good fortune, and good advice, brought her Marie Rodell, who had been a writer and editor before she became an agent. Not only did Rodell and Carson understand each other professionally, but they also became close friends.

As for finding a publisher, Simon and Schuster was not an option. There had been disappointment on both sides about *Under the Sea-Wind*, and Howe no longer worked there. Another publisher said that the outline and single chapter submitted for the new book did not give enough information on which to base a decision. Although she and Rodell were disappointed, Carson rose to the challenge. She returned to her nighttime writing, and after four months, she had written a rough draft of nearly one-third of the book. She revised it a few more times and then asked Rodell to submit it to publishers again. This time Oxford University Press said yes—offering her a contract and a cash advance. That was the vote of confidence, and the boost to her bank account, that she needed to get to work in earnest.

Underwater and Above the Waves

When Carson told Beebe about her newest project, he was enthusiastic. He had already shown his admiration for her literary gifts by including excerpts from *Under the Sea-Wind* in his *Book of Naturalists*, an anthology of what he considered the best of nature writing. Still, he told her, she should not consider going on with this new project without getting her head wet by going underwater.

Dr. William Beebe was one of the pioneers of deep-sea diving. In 1934, he and a man named Otis Barton descended far deeper below the surface than any humans had ever gone. Enclosed in a chamber called a bathysphere, the two men reached a depth of 3,028 feet, or more than 500 fathoms (a fathom is 6 feet). Beebe was not suggesting such a deep dive for Carson, but he promised to provide her with a diving helmet and weighted boots—equipment necessary for a descent of 15 feet.

Despite her love affair with the sea, Carson was not an expert swimmer, and she had had no firsthand experience of the world beneath the waves. In July 1949, however, Beebe took her on what she called "The Great Undersea Adventure," off the east coast of Florida. What she saw was a revelation. As she wrote in *The Sea Around Us*, "There I learned what the surface of the water looks like from underneath and how exquisitely delicate and varied are the colors

In July 1949, encouraged by William Beebe, Carson went to Florida to take her first dive. Here, she sits on a research boat with a diving helmet.

displayed by the animals of the reef, and I got the feeling of the misty green vistas of a strange, nonhuman world."

Her next field trip was even more challenging. Through her work at the Service, Rachel was able to spend ten days aboard a research vessel, the *Albatross III*, as it surveyed the vast Georges Bank fishing grounds off the coast of New England. It took some persuasion to get onboard, with Carson asserting that she could do her work better with first-hand knowledge of the *Albatross*'s mission, and the captain of the *Albatross* insisting that a lone woman on a working vessel with 50 crewmen was highly irregular, and bad luck to boot. Carson proposed bringing along Marie Rodell, so there would be two women, and the captain finally agreed. They set sail from Woods Hole on July 27, 1949.

Georges Bank is one of the world's most important fishing grounds. It is visited by trawlers (fishing boats) from many nations. It is actually a submerged landmass that rises like a mountain under the waves of the North Atlantic. As Carson explained it, many species seemed to be nearly fished out, and the Fish and Wildlife Service needed to find out why. The *Albatross* traversed the area, dropping nets at various points and to various depths to compile a census based on what was hauled in.

Carson and Rodell were teased by the crew members, who warned them about seasickness, bad food, accidental injuries, and other perils of a deep-sea voyage. The women endured the seasickness as the boat rolled on the open sea and soon learned to sleep through the all-night crash and clatter of the machines that reeled in the huge nets. All in all, it was a great adventure, and it gave Carson more valuable information about what lay beneath the waves. What stayed with her, once again, was a sense of wonder.

Back to the Typewriter

Thanks to Beebe, Carson got a financial boost during this period. Through his recommendation and that of several other people, she was awarded a Eugene F. Saxton Memorial Fellowship: $2,250 intended to assist writers in worthwhile, though possibly not profitable, projects. That allowed her to take a one-month leave of absence from her government job, time that she sorely needed to work on her manuscript.

Also at this time Carson had family problems to cope with. Her mother's increasing age and the illness of one of her nieces created time-consuming duties that required her attention. Shortly after she returned from Georges Bank, the family moved to a new house in Silver Spring. The move took much of Carson's precious time and energy. And, of course, her regular work had piled up in her office during her absence.

In her usual slow and meticulous fashion, Carson wrote and rewrote long into the night after hard days at the office. She suffered under the pressure, especially because—she complained to Marie Rodell—the work left her little time for bird walks and other outdoor activities. She lamented missing the spring, a favorite season. Finally, in July 1950, the manuscript was finished and mailed off to Oxford University Press. Although she did not know it at the time, she was about to become famous.

TALES
OF THE
SEA

When Rachel Carson sent the manuscript of *The Sea Around Us* to her publisher, the long days and nights of toil were behind her at last. But she was less relieved than she had expected to be. Perhaps she realized that her work was far from over. As an experienced editor in her own right, Carson involved herself deeply in the publishing process of her book. She read the edited manuscript and the galleys (long typeset pages that begin to resemble the book as it will be printed). She even gave her opinions—sometimes very strong ones—about the design of the book. She did not want it to look like a textbook or a technical publication, so she had very firm ideas about the size and style of the type used and the way pages should be arranged.

The Public Gets a Preview

Even before *The Sea Around Us* was published in July 1951, the public got a peek at the secrets of the undersea world that Carson had worked so long to chronicle. Following common practice in the publishing world, Marie Rodell launched a campaign to sell first serial rights. This meant selling the right to publish parts of the book in magazines before the book could be bought in bookstores. Serial publication is a way to give readers a preview—to whet their appetites for the main dish—and also for author and publisher to earn additional money.

Thus, in September 1950, the *Yale Review* published the chapter called "Birth of an Island," which explained how undersea volcanic eruptions formed islands such as Bermuda, Ascension, and the Hawaiian island group. That excerpt was recognized as "the finest example of science writing in an American magazine in 1950" by the American Association for the Advancement of Science, which gave Carson the George Westinghouse Science Writing Award and prize money of $1,000.

In October of that year, *Science Digest* ran another chapter, "Wealth from the Salt Seas," which talked about the enormously valuable mineral deposits in the world's oceans. In May 1951, shortly before publication day, *Nature* magazine carried the chapter entitled "The Shape of Ancient Seas," which explained how such forces of nature as ice ages, erosion, and shifting of the Earth's crust have caused sea levels to rise and fall over the course of millions of years. In it, readers learned that the lofty Himalaya Mountains were once partially submerged and that a vast inland sea once covered as much as half of the North American continent, from the Arctic to the Gulf of Mexico. Other excerpts eventually appeared in *Atlantic Naturalist* and even in the women's fashion magazine *Vogue*.

Perhaps the most exciting serial-rights sale was the one made to *The New Yorker* magazine. That famous and well-respected publication was responsible for bringing Carson's words to the attention of an enormous book-buying public.

The New Yorker's publication of "Profile of the Sea" played a huge part in the success of *The Sea Around Us*.

Feb. 26, 1949   THE   Price 20 cents

NEW YORKER

There can be no doubt that the success of the book was due, in no small part, to that single preview. *The New Yorker* ended up printing almost half of the book, in three consecutive issues, under the title "Profile of the Sea." Some might think that making so much of the book available to readers would discourage sales, but it had the opposite effect. People were so excited by what they read that they wanted to read the whole thing. They wanted to own the book to reread and refer to later.

For Rachel Carson, it also meant more money than she had ever earned before. Her income from *The New Yorker* was as much as she earned in a whole year from her government job.

Making a Splash

Two weeks before the book was published, Carson took a well-earned vacation at the beach in Beaufort, North Carolina, where she simply basked in the glories of nature, exploring tide pools and climbing on rocks just for the joy of it. Perhaps she knew that her very private life was about to be invaded.

She returned to Washington, D.C., in time for a big publication party given by her publisher. And in time for the recognition that followed.

The Saturday Review of Literature put Carson's picture on its cover. Numerous other magazines and newspapers ran glowing reviews, the Book-of-the-Month Club made *The Sea Around Us* an alternate selection, and the book was abridged in *Reader's Digest*. From the beginning, the book sold extremely well, surprising Oxford University Press, which had not printed enough copies to keep up with demand. Two months after publication, it hit the number-one spot on *The New York Times* best-seller list, where it remained for 39 weeks. All in all, it was a *Times* best-seller for 86 weeks. By the end of the year, well over 100,000 copies had been sold. A year later, sales would rise to a quarter of a million copies, an astounding number for a nonfiction book.

The book's appeal was not limited to the English-speaking world. Publishers from France to Thailand, Sweden to Japan, bought rights to the book. In time, readers in 32 languages were able to learn about the sea around them.

Another happy consequence of the book's success was the rebirth of her earlier book with Simon and Schuster, *Under the Sea-Wind*. Now that the whole world knew Rachel Carson and was eager to buy everything she wrote, Oxford University Press obtained the rights to the book from Simon and Schuster and reissued it in 1952. It, too, became a best-seller, and for a while, two books by Carson were on the best-seller list at the same time.

In addition to splendid reviews and record-breaking sales, *The Sea Around Us* began earning awards. First came the John Burroughs Medal for the year's book of outstanding literary quality in the field of natural history. That was followed by the National Book Award for the best nonfiction book of the previous year. Then came the Henry G. Bryant medal of the Philadelphia Geographical Society, awarded to a woman for the first time in the society's history. Pennsylvania College for Women, which was soon to change its name to Chatham College, gave her the honorary degree of Doctor of Literature, and Oberlin College in Ohio gave her the honorary degree of Doctor of Science. She was honored by the Drexel Institute of Technology in Philadelphia

Rachel Carson (far right) joined other National Book Award winners at the ceremony in 1951.

and was elected to the National Academy of Arts and Letters. She was even given the honor of being named a Fellow of Great Britain's Royal Society of Literature.

If Carson was delighted with the wide audience she was reaching, she was also horrified by some of the consequences of her fame. The success of her book made her a public figure—an uncomfortable situation for such a private person.

THE PRICE OF FAME

Rachel Carson was exhausted. Her mailbox was jammed with letters from fans around the world, and she considered it a point of honor to answer each personally. She had traveled and given speeches and interviews until she was worn out. She was accosted by strangers everywhere she went.

Once, in the early hours of the morning, an autograph hound knocked on the door of the motel where she and her mother were staying, and another time a fan approached her while she was under the hair dryer at a local beauty shop!

Even Hollywood came calling, with the idea of filming a documentary based on Carson's book. The movie was eventually made, and in 1953, it won an Academy Award for the best full-length documentary of the year. Nonetheless, Carson hated the film. She thought that it was oversimplified and full of distortions, and that it was also filled with out-and-out scientific errors.

What she really wanted to do was get back to work. She had research to do and another book already in mind.

The Edge of the Sea

Carson's new book, which she had started planning even before she finished the manuscript of *The Sea Around Us*, was intended to be a companion piece to her previous two books. *Under the Sea-Wind* described the lives of creatures of the sea. *The Sea Around Us* explored the physical world of the oceans—the undersea mountains and valleys, the natural forces of tides, waves, and currents. Her new book, which was eventually called *The Edge of the Sea*, would examine the extraordinary variety of life forms that live along the shore.

Carson was drawn to the shore as a subject not only because it was a place that most people could visit (in contrast to the ocean depths of her previous book) but also because of its dramatic beauty.

As always, Carson was thinking in ecological terms. She would explore the shoreline as an ecosystem and focus on how each living thing interacted with other things in its environment.

The original idea for the book had been less ambitious. While she was still working on *The Sea Around Us*, Carson had been approached by Paul Brooks, an editor at the Boston publisher Houghton Mifflin, to write a field guide to the shore. He was looking for a fairly standard type of book, with the suggested title *Guide to Seashore Life on the Atlantic Coast*, which would help beachcombers identify the creatures that they saw. But Carson certainly was not a "fairly standard" kind of writer, and she had a grander plan. She wanted to convey the marvel and complexity of the shore and its creatures.

Outdoors Again

The new book would require no less research than *The Sea Around Us* had, but much of its information would be gathered through direct observation: wading through tide pools, wandering along beaches, scooping up pails full of teeming life and examining it under magnifying glass and microscope. It was the sort of work Carson adored, but it took time—time that she simply did not have while she was working at the Service.

She applied for, and won, a Guggenheim Foundation Fellowship, which gave her money to live on while she researched the book. In June 1951, just a month before *The Sea Around Us* was published, she took a year's leave of absence from her government job. Her plan was to work full-time on the new book, but, of course, her fame intervened. She had to balance the demands of being "Rachel

Carson spent a lot of time observing the life she talked about in her books. Here, she looks through a microscope in 1951.

Carson, Famous Author" with her schedule for working on the new book. In the process, time with friends and family, and time for quiet contemplation, took a back seat.

Nonetheless, she began wading into her research, often accompanied by Bob Hines, whom she had met and supervised as a staff artist at the Service. In 1948, when Hines came to the Service, he was less than enthusiastic about having a female boss, but he came to respect Carson as a professional and to love her as a friend. He was delighted when she asked him to do the illustrations for *The Edge of the Sea*. In all, 160 of Hines's black-and-white drawings would be included in the book, and Carson took special pains to see that he received the credit he deserved for his important contribution. (In 1991, Rachel's first book, *Under the Sea-Wind*, was brought out in a special 50th anniversary edition, with illustrations by Bob Hines. We can imagine that Carson would have been pleased. Hines himself died in 1994.)

Carson insisted that Hines observe the creatures that he would illustrate in their natural habitat, rather than drawing them from preserved specimens. This meant that he had to wade in alongside her, a project he found as pleasurable as it was educational. Hines noted that Carson's sense of humor was often on display, as she sometimes commented that a certain crab looked like an acquaintance of theirs.

In the summer of 1951, Hines traveled with Carson and her mother to the Maine seacoast, where they rented a small cottage near Boothbay Harbor. Many days found them at Pemaquid, following the tides that brought in a wealth of sea life, depositing starfish, sea urchins, sponges, anemones, crabs, and tiny fish in pools left in the craggy rocks. Carson told Hines that low tides were for watching, high tides for listening. Anyone who has stood on Pemaquid Point knows

Tide pools cover the rocky shore near Pemaquid
Head Lighthouse on the coast of Maine.

what she meant; those who have not will learn that and
more by reading *The Edge of the Sea.*

Hines is the source of an often-told story of Carson, up to
her waist as usual in the icy Maine water for hours on end.
On the day in question, she had stayed in so long that her
legs were numb and she was unable to climb out. Hines had
to pluck her from the water and carry her back to the car,
where Maria Carson was waiting with a blanket to wrap
around her chilled daughter.

Hines and Carson spent their days collecting specimens,
and then, when the study and drawing were finished, they
returned the plants or animals back to the spot where they
had found them. Carson's reverence for life demanded that
the specimens be treated with respect.

Although Carson had loved Maine for many years, the
experience of that summer convinced her to make it her
home. She left the rented cottage with regret but promised
herself that she would find a way to return for a much

longer stay. She eventually did, building a cottage on Southport Island in 1953 and spending as much as six months a year there for the remainder of her life.

___

Goodbye to the Service

The plan of Carson's third book revolved around three shoreline ecosystems: the rocky shores of New England, where tides are the governing force of nature; the sandy shoals of the mid-Atlantic region, where waves sculpt the landscape and shape living conditions; and the coral and mangrove coastline of the deep South, where warm ocean currents sway.

Carson spent her leave-of-absence year visiting these locales, traveling more than 2,000 miles along the Atlantic coast. Her mother, though in her 80s, came along, as did Carson's cat, Muffin. She also returned to Woods Hole and the wonderful library at the Marine Biological Laboratory.

In June 1952, just before her leave-of-absence year was up, Carson made a momentous decision: She decided to resign her government job and devote herself full-time to writing. It was something that she had dreamed of doing for many years, but the need for a reliable income had prevented her from taking that step. Now, with *The Sea Around Us* giving her an income far beyond her wildest dreams, she finally had that freedom.

She did something else rather unusual, though anyone who knew Carson would not have been surprised by her action. She returned the Guggenheim Fellowship prize money since she no longer required that extra boost to support her writing projects.

The Rachel Carson National Wildlife Refuge

Rachel Carson's name lives on in the state of Maine through the Rachel Carson National Wildlife Refuge, which hopscotches along 45 miles of the coastline. In 1970, U.S. Secretary of the Interior Warren Hickle dedicated a stretch of Maine's shore to the memory of Rachel Carson. It had been established three years earlier as the Coastal Maine National Wildlife Refuge, one of more than 500 refuges nationwide administered by the U.S. Fish and Wildlife Service to protect wildlife and its habitats.

The fabled rocky coast of Maine is no stranger to commercial development. Motels, restaurants, and other businesses, condominiums and private houses, and the roads needed to carry hundreds of thousands of visitors there, have cut their way through the marshlands that are home to birds and many other creatures of the land and sea. In her lifetime, Carson tried to save some of those wild places from developers, helping to found the Maine chapter of the Nature Conservancy and working with that group to buy up parcels of land as a way of protecting them. These efforts were largely unsuccessful.

The land now protected by the Fish and Wildlife Service is a series of ten small areas totaling 4,600 acres dotted through vacationland Maine. It begins at Kittery, at Maine's southern border, and ends 45 miles up the coast, at Cape Elizabeth. Within the refuges more than 250 species of birds, from bitterns to sharp-shinned hawks, red-throated loons to great horned owls, coexist in an unspoiled environment

Leaving her government job marked the end of an era, not only for Carson but for the Service as well. Things had been changing there, and not for the better. The 1950s were a low point for conservationists. The country was more interested in human progress and cared little about the expense to nature. Two men whom Carson respected highly—the with white-tailed deer, weasels, river otters, mink, brook trout, and numerous other animals and plants.

The refuge's headquarters are in Wells. There, visitors can take a one-mile self-guided walk through a salt marsh, a fragile yet ever-changing ecosystem. Flooded twice a day by tidal creeks, the marsh is a mixture of freshwater and seawater that supports a complex population of marine life.

For information about visiting, contact Refuge Manager, Rachel Carson National Wildlife Refuge, R.R. 2, Box 751, Rt. 9 East, Wells, Maine 04090; telephone 207-646-9226.

Visitors can tour a salt marsh at the Rachel Carson Wildlife Refuge.

director of the Fish and Wildlife Service and the head of the Bureau of Land Management—were fired and replaced by individuals who were believed to be less committed to protecting the environment. Carson wrote an angry letter, which was published in the August 1953 edition of *Reader's Digest*. It said in part:

These actions strongly suggest that the way is being cleared for a raid upon our natural resources....The real wealth of the Nation lies in the resources of the earth—soil, water, forests, minerals, and wildlife....For many years public-spirited citizens throughout the country have been working for the conservation of the national resources....Apparently their hard-won progress is to be wiped out, as a politically minded Administration returns us to the dark ages of unrestrained exploitation and destruction. It is one of the ironies of our time, that, while concentrating on the defense of our country against enemies from without, we should be so heedless of those who would destroy it from within.

Although Rachel Carson's words are nearly a half century old, they are as up-to-date as today's headlines.

The Friendship of a Lifetime

One day in December 1952, Carson received a letter from a Maine neighbor. Carson had picked out a piece of land on a wooded bluff overlooking a rocky beach on Southport Island. A small cottage was being built there, and she hoped that it would be ready by the following summer. Her neighbor, Dorothy Freeman, was writing to welcome her to the area and to express her admiration for *The Sea Around Us*, which Freeman's husband, Stanley, had received as a birthday present. Carson wrote back, inviting the Freemans to come visit once she and her mother had settled in.

With that simple exchange of polite letters, one of the most important friendship of Carson's life began. Rachel and Dorothy became the dearest of friends, spending much of their time in Maine together and exchanging letters, sometimes daily, over the course of the next 11 years.

In Freeman, Carson felt that she had, for the first time in her life, met someone who understood both the writer and the person that she was.

They shared a love of nature in general, of the Maine seacoast in particular, and a devotion to family and friends. They talked and wrote to each other about the books they had read, the birds they had seen, and what the tide brought in, about family illnesses and difficulties, about Carson's

Rachel Carson explored the tide pools near her home in Maine.

cats and her agonies of creation while she was writing a book, about the change of seasons, and so much more. Rachel felt that she and Dorothy were kindred spirits. She considered herself lucky to have found such a friend. Rachel found in Dorothy someone who could share her triumphs and her tragedies, the brightest and darkest of her days. In the last decade of her life, she had more than her share of all these things.

Bright Days, and Dark

When it was published in 1955, *The Edge of the Sea* was dedicated to "Dorothy and Stanley Freeman, who have gone with me to the low-tide world and have felt its beauty and its mystery." Although it did not make as big a splash as *The Sea Around Us*, it received excellent reviews and spent 23 weeks on the best-seller list. Once again, *The New Yorker* carried lengthy excerpts, and *Reader's Digest* featured a condensed version. More honors and awards followed, from such groups as the American Association of University Women and the National Council of Women of the United States. Smith College granted Carson an honorary doctoral degree.

Although she did not have a new book in the works, Carson continued to write. She even ventured into the relatively new medium of television, writing the script for a program on clouds entitled "Something About the Sky," which was broadcast in 1956.

Carson and her mother divided their time between Silver Spring, Maryland, and Southport Island, Maine, arriving at their Maine cottage as early as possible in the spring and staying as late as they could in the fall. Rachel's nieces had long since grown and married, and Maria Carson's health was beginning to fail. Now in her late 80s, she had arthritis, a painful and debilitating disease that seemed to run in the family. She was further weakened by a bout of pneumonia in December 1956.

With her concern focused on her mother's health, Carson was stunned when, two months later, her niece Marjorie died of pneumonia. As Carson had done for "Marjie" and her sister Marian 20 years before, she now took in Marjie's young son Roger, adopting the five-year old boy when she herself was 50.

This time, at least, money was not a problem when the family expanded. Carson was able to build a new house in Silver Spring and to give Roger a comfortable and secure home in which to grow up. And if she seemed too old to be the mother of such a young child, we must remember "Help Your Child to Wonder," the 1956 magazine article—later a book—that Carson wrote based on her experience of sharing nature with Roger. The boy had been a frequent visitor to Southport Island while his mother was alive; now, it had become his home.

Carson's greatest loss came less than two years later, on December 1, 1958, when her mother died at the age of 89. The woman who had introduced her to the natural world and had stood by her side as she grew from child to woman was gone.

HER
MIGHTY
PEN

One January day in 1958, Rachel Carson's mailbox held an envelope from a friend. Olga Owens Huckins was distressed about the robins that were dying in her backyard bird sanctuary in Duxbury, Massachusetts. Huckins enclosed a letter that she had written to *The Boston Herald* newspaper. According to the letter, the state of Massachusetts had conducted an aerial spraying program against mosquitoes, blanketing the area with the insecticide DDT. The day the plane went over, she noticed seven dead birds in her yard; the day after that, three more corpses lay at her back door, "Their bills gaping open and their splayed claws...drawn up to their breasts in agony." The next day, there were three more dead, and the following day, a bird perched in a tree keeled over and died at her feet.

Huckins was writing for Carson's advice: How could she find out more about this deadly chemical? If it was killing songbirds, what effect was it having on humans and other living things in the vicinity? How long would the poison last? Was there any way to stop what she called the "serious aerial intrusion"?

When people talk about the origins of *Silent Spring*, they often tell this story, suggesting it was Huckins's letter that planted the idea in Carson's mind to write a book about the dangers of pesticides. In fact, Carson had been concerned about the issue since her days at the Fish and Wildlife Service during World War II, and she had even tried to do something about it then. Huckins's letter was not news to Carson, though it was probably the signal that the time to act had come.

What Is DDT?

DDT is an acronym for dichloro-diphenyl-trichloroethane, a chlorinated hydrocarbon (or organochloride) insect killer that was once hailed as a miracle of modern science. It was first synthesized in 1874 by Othmar Ziedler, a pharmacist in Vienna, Austria. But it was not used as an insecticide until 1940, when a patent was granted to Paul H. Muller, an employee of the Swiss chemical and pharmaceutical firm Geigy. The discovery was considered so important that Muller was awarded the Nobel Prize in Physiology or Medicine in 1948.

Before that time, humankind was relatively helpless in combating the insect pests that are responsible for destroying food crops by the thousands of acres and, perhaps more serious, for carrying such deadly human diseases as malaria, plague (a highly infectious bacterial disease), and typhus. Geigy hoped to find a substance to kill clothes moths, but the U.S. Army was more interested in protecting soldiers from insect-borne diseases.

After the war, DDT and its "cousins" in the organochloride family (dieldrin, endrin, chlordane, and others) were made available for civilian use, so that the once-again prosperous country could benefit from these miraculous new chemicals. Production of synthetic (humanmade) pesticides increased fivefold between 1947 and 1960, with more than 600 million pounds produced in 1960 alone.

For the manufacturers, pesticides were big business, bringing them millions of dollars in profits each year. For farmers, too, they were an economic miracle, protecting their crops and enabling them to produce food for a growing nation as well as for export to the hungry world. Anyone who suggested that there was a dark side to the pesticide use would be battling these powerful business interests and the politicians who served them.

THE DARK SIDE

There was another side to the story, and it was very dark indeed. Whether you care about the health of the Earth as a whole or just about the human population, DDT and the other synthetic pesticides represent a serious danger.

The very things that make them so attractive to their manufacturers and users also make them perilous: They are relatively cheap and easy to manufacture, and they stay in the environment a very long time. Furthermore, they are

DDT was sprayed from planes onto crops.

broad-spectrum poisons, which means that they are effective against many different insect species. As a result, beneficial insects are killed along with harmful ones. In the web of life that Carson so revered, many species of insects are helpful to humankind. Ladybugs and praying mantises, for example, eat many of the insects that feed on crops. Bees and butterflies perform vital roles in plant reproduction, by carrying pollen from flowering plants.

Pesticides are applied through spraying, which means that many of the chemicals end up in the air we breathe as

Poison in the Food Chain

The food chain represents the system by which organisms in an ecosystem feed—the network of who eats what or whom. It is described in terms of levels. Members of one level feed on members of the level below them. In turn, they are fed upon by members of the level above them. As a simplified example, plankton are eaten by small fish, which are eaten by larger fish, which are eaten by people.

A food web is a combination of linked food chains within a particular ecosystem. For example, the plankton are also eaten by whales in a separate chain; and the larger fish are also eaten by seabirds or by seals, in other chains. All of these chains are part of a large, complex food web.

In general, plants are at the bottom of the food chain, and humans and other higher mammals are at the top. Although it might sound like an advantage to be at or near the top of a food chain, creatures at the top of the food chain face their own particular kinds of life-threatening hazards.

When poisons enter the food chain, they may be passed along from one level to the next. This is the case with organochloride pesticides and many other pollutants. Rather than degrading (disintegrating harmlessly), they multiply, gaining in concentration (potency) at each successive level. Therefore, the higher up on the food chain the pollutants go, the greater the concentration of their poisons become.

DDT and the other organochlorides are fat-soluble. This means that they do not dissolve in water. Therefore, they are not eliminated from the body through urine. Instead, they are stored in the fatty tissues

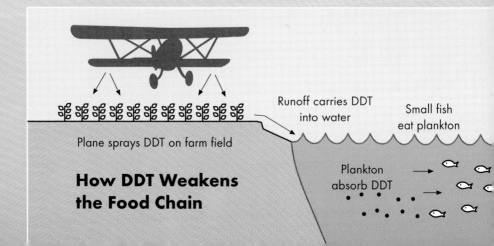

Plane sprays DDT on farm field

Runoff carries DDT into water

Small fish eat plankton

Plankton absorb DDT

How DDT Weakens the Food Chain

and organs of fish, birds, and mammals. When a fish eats a smaller fish that has fed on plankton that has absorbed DDT from the surrounding water, the larger fish picks up the dose gathered by each of the previous links in the chain. When a human eats that larger fish, the accumulated DDT is part of the meal. The fish protein may be digested and the waste eliminated, but DDT remains in the body. Over time, DDT can cause cancer, damage the immune and nervous systems and the liver, contribute to birth defects, disrupt the normal action of hormones, and increase the harmful effects of other poisons.

DDT has a particularly damaging effect on birds. Among other things, it disrupts their metabolism. They become starved of calcium. To make up for this, they smash and eat their own eggs, which are rich in calcium. The calcium deficiency also makes the eggshells very fragile—so fragile that most do not survive to hatch. In California, the eggs of brown pelicans have been found to be so flimsy that they break when nesting birds sit on them. The result has endangered many bird species, among them the golden eagle and the peregrine falcon.

Living thousands of miles away from, or even decades after, where and when DDT has been used does not prevent an organism from feeding on the poison. Rachel Carson's *Silent Spring* prompted President John F. Kennedy to appoint a special commission to research DDT. This collective effort resulted in the banning of DDT in 1972. More than 20 years later traces have been found in the Arctic region, in tissues of wildlife and in the breast milk of human women. In Antarctica, DDT has been found in the flesh of seals, penguins, and storm petrels. In the oceans, the livers of many fish and the flesh of such fatty fish as mackerel have been found to be tainted with DDT.

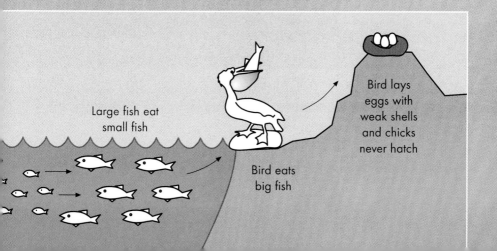

Large fish eat small fish

Bird eats big fish

Bird lays eggs with weak shells and chicks never hatch

well as returning to the ground when it rains or snows, often many miles from where they were originally sprayed. Air currents in the upper atmosphere carry the poisons around the globe. The residue on the plants and in the soil finds its way into the groundwater that we drink, and it runs off into rivers, where it kills fish and other water-dwelling creatures. Eventually, it ends up in the oceans, where it is picked up by both plant and animal species living there. In all of these ways, it ends up in the food chain, coming back to haunt humankind for untold years.

The First Alarm

It was in the course of her work at the Fish and Wildlife Service that Carson first learned about DDT. Powdered DDT was used by the military in Italy during World War II to combat the insect-borne disease typhus, which was killing American soldiers in great numbers. In 1945, the government decided to conduct a series of tests to find out how the widespread use of DDT would affect the delicate balance of the environment.

Carson was interested in these same problems, and concerned. She wrote a letter to *Reader's Digest*, proposing an article about the government tests. Even then, Carson suspected that the more that was learned about the ecological impact of this humanmade chemical, the clearer it would be that its dangers far outweighed its benefits.

Unfortunately, *Reader's Digest* was not interested in publishing an article on the subject. Rachel had other things to do, so she filed the idea away—that is, until she received Huckins's letter, 13 years later.

An Idea Whose Time Had Come

Rachel began asking around for answers to Huckins's questions, and the more she found out, the more disturbed she became. Massachusetts was not the only place where pesticide spraying was taking place. Widespread aerial spraying was used all across the country, with little thought given to the long-term effects—on people as well as the environment. She and Huckins were not alone in their concerns: One group of citizens was even planning to go to court to stop the spraying.

Pollution occurs in many forms. This fish has suffocated from over-production of algae, probably due to fertilizer run-off in the area.

In 1957, a massive spraying program had drenched a suburban area on Long Island with DDT mixed with fuel oil (to make it stick to plants and other surfaces) in an effort to combat the tree-damaging gypsy moths. The poison rained down on vegetable and dairy farms, backyard gardens and school playgrounds. Flowers and shrubs were destroyed, automobiles were damaged, and many living things—from insects and birds to a horse—were killed.

Carson thought that it was important to inform the public about the dangers of such programs, so she asked her agent Marie Rodell if she knew of any writers with the interest, and the expertise, to write a magazine article or even a book about the new pesticides. It soon became clear, however, that if anyone would and could write it, it was Carson herself.

She went back to *Reader's Digest*, which to her dismay was actually planning an article on the benefits of aerial spraying, and asked the magazine if it would be willing to publish her opposing view. *Reader's Digest* turned her down, as did several other magazines to which Carson made the proposal. One of them, *Good Housekeeping*, even made the argument that publishing such an article would unnecessarily panic its readers.

Carson saw the coming court trial on Long Island as an opportunity. She wrote to E. B. White, the author of the children's classic *Charlotte's Web* and an editor at *The New Yorker*, suggesting that he cover the trial for the magazine. White wrote back saying that he could not because personal business would keep him at home in Maine, and he urged Carson to write the article herself.

Everywhere that Carson turned, the message was the same: Yes, it is important, and you are the person to do it. Finally, she gave in. She decided to write an article for *The New Yorker* on the Long Island lawsuit, which she would then expand into a short book of essays on pesticide use and abuse.

In May 1958, she signed a contract with Houghton Mifflin for a book on pesticides. She expected to finish it less than two months later and to publish it early in 1959. In fact, it would be four years, and many thousands of hours of research later, before the message of *Silent Spring* was heard loud and clear across the land.

A Moral Issue

For Carson, the misuse of pesticides was a moral issue. Do humans have a right to tamper with the balance of nature? Do they have a right to put their interests before those of other living things with whom they share the Earth? Do they have a right to introduce such "marvelous" new discoveries as pesticides, nuclear energy, and even antibiotic medicines without studying their long-term effects on the environment as a whole?

Carson took a long view; she considered the millions of years of the Earth's existence, not merely the thousands of years of human civilization. It is no surprise that she approached her newest project from an ecological standpoint, just as she had all her previous work. And from that standpoint, Carson saw humankind as the most destructive "pest" of all.

She knew, however, that in order to wage a moral battle, she had to arm herself with facts. She marshaled all of her energy and all of her resources to do just that. The solid training in research that she had acquired at Johns Hopkins University and refined during her years at the Service came in handy. So did her many contacts in the scientific community. Carson's fame as author of *The Sea Around Us,* and the respect that so many people had for her, worked in her favor as well.

About a year into the project, she hired a research assistant, Jeanne Davis, who helped her obtain and digest the enormous amount of information she needed. With Davis's assistance, Carson wrote to experts around the world and read mountains of books and scientific papers on subjects

Pesticide Tolerance

One of the greatest ironies of widespread pesticide use is that the very insects that we want to kill become immune to the poisons fairly quickly. How they do this is not absolutely clear, but one of the explanations is that they develop chemicals in their bodies to neutralize the toxic effects. Those that survive breed again, passing on to the next generation this resistance to the pesticides. Soon, a "super-race" of insects is established that is not affected by the pesticides, and newer, more powerful and dangerous pesticides must be developed in order to kill them.

This happened with DDT, which was once called the answer to the deadly disease malaria. Between 1956 and 1969, the United States contributed nearly $800 million to the Global Eradication of Malaria Program. By the end of that time, the mosquitoes that carry malaria had developed resistance to DDT. Today, more than 150 species of insect pests are immune to the spray of what was once considered a miracle of modern science.

A similar problem has developed with many disease-causing bacteria. Antibiotic medicines have been a powerful weapon against these organisms for the past half century. Many deadly infections, including tuberculosis, were thought to be conquered, saving millions of human lives. Now, however, medical scientists are discovering that many of the most deadly bacteria have developed immunity to the strongest antibiotics we have. The very miracle that was used to fight disease has created a generation of "super-germs," leaving humankind vulnerable to diseases we thought had been conquered.

as diverse as agronomy, medicine, biochemistry, organic chemistry, and land use. So extensive was her research that the list of principal sources that she consulted occupies 54 pages at the end of *Silent Spring*.

A Valiant Spirit in a Fragile Body

When it came to writing the book, Carson faced more than her usual difficulty with getting words on paper. This time, she needed to explain a complicated topic in terms that ordinary people could understand. And she needed to keep them interested, despite the dry and depressing nature of the material. She labored intensely to strike just the right balance. Although *Silent Spring* can be heavy reading in parts, it is full of information told in terms that a nonscientist can understand. As with all her writings, it was a work of literature.

Carson faced other difficulties, however, having to do with her health. Since childhood, she had been physically fragile, vulnerable to colds and other viruses that seemed to hang on longer than they did for most people. As an adult, she developed arthritis, as her mother and her niece Marjorie had. Lately, Carson had found just moving around to be quite painful. In the spring of 1960, she had a bout of flu that led to a serious sinus infection. No sooner had that cleared up than she developed an ulcer, a painful stomach disorder. Not long after that, she had breast surgery, though the doctor who removed a suspicious lump told her the entire tumor had been removed and that it had not, in any event, been cancerous. It was not until the end of the year that she learned the truth. It was cancer, and there were signs that it had spread.

Carson began a series of radiation treatments in hopes of stopping the cancer. Such treatments often result in the loss of hair, extreme tiredness, and a weakening of the body's immune system, which works to fight off illness and disease. Carson was subject to all of the above. She bought a wig to camouflage her hair loss and tried to work through the fatigue, often doing her writing in bed, but she was unable to fight off a serious bacterial infection in her legs. For a while, she was confined to her bed or a wheelchair and needed the services of a nurse around the clock. After that infection had cleared up, she had an eye infection that left her without useful vision for more than three weeks.

Carson worried about her progress on the book, but even more about her grandnephew Roger, then ten years old, who needed her loving attention more than ever. All things considered, it is a small miracle that she was able to finish the manuscript and send it off to her editor, Paul Brooks, in January 1962.

THE WORLD DISCOVERS SILENT SPRING

In a now-familiar pattern, parts of Rachel Carson's book first appeared in *The New Yorker*: Nearly one third of the manuscript was published in three weekly installments, beginning on June 16, 1962. Houghton Mifflin had set publication for late September.

As soon as *The New Yorker* excerpts appeared, a firestorm erupted. Readers were so outraged by the facts that Carson had assembled that they wrote, not only to her and *The New Yorker*, but also to their elected government representatives and to heads of government agencies. Magazines and newspapers published a flood of letters to the editor, columns, and editorial cartoons. The reaction mainly favored Carson's point of view. However, there were powerful people—and corporations—that opposed it. Simply put, it was a war between economics and ecology. The battle lines had been drawn.

Business interests and farmers attacked Carson and the contents of *Silent Spring*, claiming that the author was unqualified to discuss pesticides, and the book was inaccurate.

The Chemical Counterattack

The first attack came even before the book was published. The Velsicol Corporation, manufacturer of the organochloride pesticide chlordane, tried to prevent Houghton Mifflin from bringing out the book. It threatened a lawsuit based on what it called inaccuracies. The publisher had the book examined by an expert, who found it accurate. Houghton Mifflin refused to be pressured and promised that the book would be published without any changes. Velsicol dropped its threat, and the book was published on September 27, 1962. Within two weeks, it was on *The New York Times* bestseller list, and Rachel Carson was once again in the news.

When Carson was doing her research, many people had warned her that she would make enemies with the project. Some chemists in government and industry agreed to help her only if their participation were kept secret: They feared for their jobs. But Carson stood by her beliefs, even when these warnings came true.

The chemical companies were enraged. Carson had attacked them in their pocketbooks, and that made them fighting mad. So were farmers, who warned that without chemical pesticides, America would go hungry. People whose business interests would be hurt by controls on pesticides called *Silent Spring* one-sided, inaccurate, hysterical, and dangerous. Without these miracle products they said, the world would return to the dark ages of the plague and other epidemics. In fact, they were the ones who were being overly dramatic. Although some of these things are caused by insects, pesticides are not the only, or even the most effective, weapon to fight them.

Much of the criticism was part of a well-planned campaign by public relations firms working for the pesticide manufacturers. One such outfit, the National Agricultural Chemicals Association, budgeted $250,000 for advertising and brochures that attempted to discredit *Silent Spring* while they promoted the wonders of a world that is protected by pesticides.

When opponents tried to discredit her book, they were unable to argue with its scientific accuracy, so they attacked the character of its author instead. The attacks claimed that Carson was not qualified to analyze the situation—that she was a marine biologist, not a chemist, a writer of books about the sea, and foolishly sentimental about animals. They misrepresented what she said and what she meant in *Silent Spring*. One critic even suggested that as a spinster (an unkind term meaning an unmarried woman), Carson had no need to worry about birth defects or the dangers of pesticides to future generations!

Carson may not have been a chemist, but she was a tireless researcher with access to experts and a keenly analytical mind. She was able to assemble the facts and back them up, and the facts spoke for themselves.

In the Spotlight—and on the Hot Seat

Imagine Rachel Carson: the shy, private person, suffering from terminal cancer, forced into the spotlight by her latest book. The celebrity of *The Sea Around Us* had been difficult enough for her, and in that case she had been overwhelmed by fans praising her. Now she was being attacked by powerful critics: influential people of industry and even of government.

Perhaps because she knew this was her final battle, she found the courage to carry on. She spoke before a special congressional committee considering the pesticide question and even agreed to face her critics on television. In April 1963, she appeared on a television program "CBS Reports: The Silent Spring of Rachel Carson." The other guests were a representative of the chemical giant American Cyanamid, the secretary of the U.S. Department of Agriculture, the head

President Kennedy was impressed by *Silent Spring* and formed a committee to study the book's claims.

On June 4, 1963, Carson testified against the use of pesticides before a Senate committee.

of the U.S. Public Health Service, and the commissioner of the U.S. Food and Drug Administration, all of them defending pesticides against her accusations. Appearing on national television with these powerful people took a lot of courage, but Carson remained calm and strong, confident of the accuracy of her book.

Despite these enemies, she also had powerful allies. President John F. Kennedy was one of the thousands who read her book, and he was impressed. He assembled a Special Panel of the President's Scientific Advisory Committee to study the issues raised by *Silent Spring*. When the Panel made its report in May 1963, it was sharply critical not only of the pesticide industry, but also of the policies of the Department of Agriculture and the Food and Drug

Administration. It credited *Silent Spring* for alerting the public to the dangers of chemical pesticides and endorsed Carson's scientific conclusions. Finally, it made a series of recommendations, the last of which was to set a future goal of eliminating the use of persistent toxic pesticides.

ANOTHER SPRING

Silent Spring brought Rachel Carson yet more awards, including the Audubon Medal. In January 1963, she was given the Schweitzer Medal of the Animal Welfare Institute, named for the renowned physician and philosopher Albert Schweitzer, whose concept of "Reverence for Life" had been a guiding principle for her.

Just a few months later, as spring was blossoming, Carson suffered a heart attack. She went to her Maine cottage to recuperate, accompanied by 11-year-old Roger and her cats. (After her death, Roger would go to live with her editor, biographer, and friend, Paul Brooks, and his wife.) Her dear friend Dorothy Freeman visited her in Maine and again when she returned to Silver Spring.

In the last letter that Dorothy received from her, Carson said: "I have had a rich life, full of rewards and satisfactions that come to few, and if it must end now, I can feel that I have achieved most of what I wished to do. That wouldn't have been true two years ago, when I first realized my time was short, and I am so grateful to have had this extra time."

Rachel Carson died on April 14, 1964, at her home in Silver Spring, Maryland.

CHAPTER SIX

THE EARTH
SHE
LEFT US

In 1972, DDT and other organochloride pesticides were banned for use in the United States, fulfilling the long-term goal set by President John F. Kennedy's Scientific Advisory Committee nearly ten years before. As important as that action was, the legacy of widespread use of this dangerous chemical is still with us. The ban on DDT is not worldwide. It is still used in many parts of the world, including Mexico. And the American chemical companies that manufacture organochloride pesticides continue to produce them for export. As Carson warned, there are no local environmental problems, only worldwide ones. Chemical pollution knows no national boundaries. Poisons in the air, oceans, and soil travel even to lands where they have been outlawed.

The Nation Takes Action

Less than a year after *Silent Spring* was published, at least 40 laws had been proposed in state legislatures to control pesticide use. On the national level, the next decade saw at least a dozen new laws to protect the environment. In 1970, the federal Environmental Protection Agency (EPA) was established, and the regulation of pesticides was transferred away from the Department of Agriculture to the EPA. Departments of environmental protection were established by every state and by many cities.

Pesticides were not the only focus of these laws and government agencies. Attention was being paid to pollution of the water, air, and soil by many other means, as well as to the need to protect wildlife habitats and endangered species, and to reduce and recycle the mountains of waste that we produce.

After the publication of *Silent Spring,* many laws were passed to stop the use of pesticides. Today, organic farms, such as this one, produce food without the use of chemicals.

On April 22, 1970, Americans celebrated the first Earth Day. It is now an annual event that combines both protests against people and policies that damage the environment and positive action to solve problems on both local and global scales.

Some people observe the day by cleaning up a local park or working in a recycling center. Others meet with lawmakers to urge stronger laws or stage demonstrations against known polluters or in favor of ecologically sound policies.

PERSISTENT POISONS

It would be a fairy-tale ending to say that the world listened to Carson's message and that all the damage that had previously been done was reversed. The real story is far different, and it has not ended yet.

Part of that story is that DDT and similar poisons are still with us. Organochlorides do not lose their toxicity as they degrade, and they degrade very slowly. It takes between 10 and 20 years for the potency of the poison to be reduced by half, and another 10 to 20 years for that half to be itself reduced by half. It is now thought that DDT residues remain poisonous for up to 50 years. Therefore, pesticides used in the United States before the 1970 ban are still present in our soil and water. According to the Environmental Protection Agency, the groundwater in at least 30 states is contaminated with as many as 50 different pesticides. Residues of many cancer-causing pesticides have been found in meat sold for public consumption.

What is more, pesticides banned in the United States that are used elsewhere in the world are capable of traveling huge distances. Recently, scientists have found traces of DDT, chlordane, aldrin, and 19 other pesticides in the bark of trees in 90 test locations around the world.

After organochlorides were banned in the United States, their job was taken by organophosphates, another type of

THE RACHEL CARSON COUNCIL

In 1965, Shirley Briggs, Rachel's good friend and coworker from the Fish and Wildlife Service, joined with other friends and supporters of Rachel's views to form the Rachel Carson Trust for the Living Environment. Now called the Rachel Carson Council, this nonprofit environmental organization publishes informational and educational materials on chemical contaminants and their alternatives. It runs special programs for young people through its Junior Rachel Carson Councils, and funds a Rachel Carson Council Junior Scholar Program, through which students do independent research on the environment. The Council is deeply concerned about the continuing dangers of pesticide use and abuse. It promotes such alternatives as biological controls and integrated pest management (IPM). For information on Council activities and publications, write to Rachel Carson Council, 8940 Jones Mill Road, Chevy Chase, MD 20815.

powerful toxin that affects the nervous system of humans and insects. Among the organophosphates currently in use are parathion and malathion. There have been many incidents of organophosphate poisoning resulting from direct exposure or from eating tainted food. For example, parathion-contaminated sugar killed 17 children in Tijuana, Mexico; 600 others were severely sickened at the same time. In Colombia, 80 people died when they ate bread made from parathion-contaminated flour. Agricultural workers in the United States are particularly vulnerable to these pesticides, since they are exposed to the sprays in the course of their work. Despite protection efforts, many illnesses and even deaths have been blamed on exposure to pesticides among people who work to put food on our dining tables.

SAFER PEST CONTROL

Even though her enemies accused Carson of caring more about bugs than people, anyone who reads *Silent Spring* knows that her criticism was constructive. She pointed out the many dangers of uncontrolled pesticide use, but she did not say that they should never be used to protect crops and people from disease and destruction. In the book's last chapter, "The Other Road," Carson explored safe alternatives to uncontrolled spraying with long-lasting poisons. She favored what has come to be called integrated pest management, or IPM. As its name suggests, IPM involves a combination of methods to control pests. Smaller amounts of chemicals can be combined with biological and physical controls to

Ladybugs can be introduced to some food crops, protecting crops from harmful insects. Here, a ladybug attacks bird-cherry aphids on a cereal leaf.

effectively protect plants and people without damaging other living things in the ecosystem. Some of the most promising biological controls include introducing beneficial insects, such as certain types of wasps and ladybugs that eat damaging insects; introducing sterile male insects, so that mating attempts will not produce a new generation; and infecting insects with bacteria and viruses that are harmless to people but kill the insects. Physical controls include changing planting patterns, forbidding the importation of agricultural products that might harbor pests from other regions of the world, and physically removing the pests from crops.

Although IPM is more complicated and usually more expensive than spraying with powerful pesticides, it has many supporters among those who want to find safe alternatives to using poisons throughout the world.

From Radicalism to Mainstream

Carson spoke up at a time when challenging government policies took a tremendous amount of courage. The McCarthy era of the 1950s—a time when disagreeing with the mainstream often meant losing one's job and reputation—was a fresh memory for most people. Within a few short years, opposition to the country's involvement in the Vietnam War would also be branded by many as treasonous. It is encouraging, therefore, that environmental activism has in our time become not only acceptable, but has even taken its place as government policy. In the mid-1990s, no less a figure than Vice-President Al Gore spoke frankly about the need to protect the environment if humankind is to have a

Al Gore (center) and actor Christopher Reeve (right) worked with volunteers who cleaned garbage from a beach in 1992. Gore credited Carson for helping to start the environmental movement.

future. He wrote a book arguing that point called *Earth in the Balance*, and he contributed the introduction to the newest edition of *Silent Spring*.

In that introduction he says: "...Rachel Carson's landmark book offers undeniable proof that the power of an idea can be far greater than the power of politicians....Without this book, the environmental movement might have been long delayed or never have developed at all."

A Continuing Struggle

Despite the influence of Carson and her writings, despite the changes in public awareness and government policy, despite the many hopeful signs that some endangered species have been saved from extinction, the battle for our planet has not been won yet. Unfortunately, there are signs that many of the efforts of the past quarter century will be put on hold.

Many individuals, organizations, and elected representatives are committed to preserving the environment, but many others are not. The same moral and scientific issues that Carson championed are under attack by powerful forces today. In recent years, environmental regulations have been weakened and public money taken away from agencies and organizations dedicated to protecting the environment. The federal Environmental Protection Agency recently set 15 long-term goals related to clean air, clean water, pollution prevention, and reduction of global environmental risks, among others. At the same time, however, the Agency's head admitted that budget cuts would make it impossible to achieve those goals. Clearly, many politicians and planners still believe that the economy is more important than environmental concerns. Every day, newspaper headlines tell of the conflict between those who believe that humankind must share the earth with other living things and those who believe that the current generation has absolute priority.

One sign of hope lies in the younger generation. Many young people believe that protecting the earth's environment is of utmost importance. They are concerned about endangered species and habitats, global warming, and destruction of the ozone layer. They support efforts to recycle and reduce waste, and to stop pollution of our precious air and water resources. They learn about the environment in school, and many participate in school and community activities that work to protect the environment. When these young people become voters, perhaps they will be able to influence lawmakers to keep environmental protection on the national agenda.

Rachel Carson

Getting Involved

When Rachel Carson wrote *Silent Spring*, there were only a handful of organizations dedicated to protecting wildlife and the environment. In the years since its publication, many new organizations have sprung up. Many are open for membership, and all will provide information to people interested in the particular issues on which they focus. Some of the major ones are:

Defenders of Wildlife
1244 19th Street, NW
Washington, D.C. 20036

Earthwatch
P. O. Box 403N
680 Mount Auburn Street
Watertown, MA 02272

Environmental Defense Fund
257 Park Avenue South
New York, NY 10010

Friends of the Earth
218 D Street, SE
Washington, D.C. 20003

Greenpeace
1432 U Street, NW
Washington, D.C. 20009

National Audubon Society
700 Broadway
New York, NY 10003

National Wildlife Federation
1412 16 Street, NW
Washington, D.C. 20036

Natural Resources Defense
  Council
40 West 20 Street
New York, NY 10011

The Nature Conservancy
1815 North Lynn Street
Arlington, VA 22209

Sierra Club
730 Polk Street
San Francisco, CA 94109

Worldwatch Institute
1776 Massachusetts Avenue,
  NW
Washington, D.C. 20036

Women in Science

When Carson switched her college major from English literature to biology, she was warned that science was a man's world. She did not let that stop her, though she faced many obstacles in her pursuit of a career as a scientist. Have things changed since Carson's time? Do young women who want to pursue careers in the sciences face the same or other obstacles, or are careers in this field now as open to women as they are to men?

There are certainly many more women working in the sciences today than there were when Carson was starting her career. Women are a common presence in many graduate science programs and medical schools, and they hold jobs in university research facilities, private industry, and government programs.

These changes did not take place overnight, nor has all prejudice against women disappeared from the field. It still takes determination to become a scientist—for women as well as men—and the day has not yet come that a woman will not have to prove herself against a higher standard than a similarly skilled man must face.

If awards are a measure of advancement in a given field, a glance at the respected Nobel Prizes in Chemistry, Physics, and Physiology or Medicine will tell us that women still have a long way to go. Since Marie Curie won the prize in 1903, only one other woman has received the Nobel in the field of physics. Maria Goeppert-Mayer shared the prize in 1963 for her work on nuclear shell structure.

In the field of chemistry, Marie Curie's daughter, Irene Joliot-Curie, shared the 1935 Nobel Prize with her husband,

Frederic Joliot, for their work on synthesizing radioactive elements. It would be nearly 30 years before another woman won a Nobel prize in chemistry. In 1964, Dorothy C. Hodgkin became only the second woman in history to win the prize in that category. Her achievement concerned a means for determining the structure of complex molecules.

One female scientist who can be viewed as the spiritual daughter of Rachel Carson is Sylvia A. Earle, a marine biologist, environmentalist, and pioneering deep-sea explorer. Once the chief scientist at the National Oceanographic and Atmospheric Administration, she is now an independent oceanographer who has gone deeper beneath the waves than Rachel Carson could ever have imagined. Earle's knowledge of and expertise in deep-ocean technology and engineering is in enormous demand.

REMEMBERING RACHEL CARSON

In his introduction to *Silent Spring*, Vice-President Al Gore said that Carson's "picture hangs on my office wall among those of the political leaders, the presidents and prime ministers. It has been there for years—and it belongs there. Carson has had as much or more effect on me than any of them, and perhaps than all of them together." Gore is not the only one who remembers Carson and the profound effect that she has had on environmental awareness. She has been honored in many ways since her death.

Perhaps the greatest honor was given in 1980, when then-President Jimmy Carter awarded her the Presidential Medal of Freedom, the highest civilian honor given by the U.S. government. In giving the award, he said:

Never silent herself in the face of destructive trends, Rachel Carson fed a spring of awareness across America and beyond. A biologist with a gentle, clear voice, she welcomed her audiences to her love of the sea, while with an equally clear determined voice, she warned Americans of the dangers human beings themselves pose for their own environment. Always concerned, always eloquent, she created a tide of environmental consciousness that has not ebbed.

Carson's adoptive son and grandnephew Roger Christie accepted the medal in her name.

The Presidential Medal of Freedom was awarded to Rachel Carson in 1980. Roger Christie accepted the medal for his grandaunt.

Through her writings, Rachel Carson shared her love of nature and appreciation of her surroundings with everyone.

In 1981, the U. S. Post Office offered a first-class stamp honoring Carson as part of its Great Americans series. Its first day of issue was May 27, her birthday, with the postmark of Springdale, Pennsylvania, her hometown.

It is also possible to visit places that memorialize Carson. In 1974, Rachel Carson Homestead Association was founded to preserve the house in Springdale, Pennsylvania, where she was born. The Homestead offers tours to individuals and groups. The Rachel Carson National Wildlife Refuge in Maine, dedicated in 1970, is also open to visitors.

Perhaps the best way to remember Carson is simply to take a walk outdoors. It could be in the woods on an autumn day or at low tide near the seashore, in a springtime meadow or on a snowy evening. You could hike to the crest of a hill or down to the banks of a river, or just venture into the world of your own backyard. You could take along binoculars and a field guide to plants, mammals, birds, or marine life, but all you really need are your five senses, plus your sense of wonder for the beauty of nature.

Glossary

aldrin An organochloride pesticide related to DDT; banned for use in the United States.

biology The scientific study of living things; includes botany and zoology and the many branches of each.

botany The scientific study of the plant kingdom.

chlordane An organochloride pesticide related to DDT; banned for use in the United States.

DDT Dichloro-diphenyl-trichloroethane, a chlorinated hydrocarbon (or organochloride) insecticide; banned for use in the United States.

dieldrin An organochloride insecticide, related to DDT; banned for use in the United States.

ecology The science of the interactions between living things and their environment.

ecosystem An entire community of living things and its environment.

food chain The order of feeding of living things within an ecosystem; who eats whom and who is eaten by whom. Plants and single-celled organisms are usually at the bottom of the food chain; humans and other large animals are usually at the top.

food web A series of overlapping and interconnected food chains

fungicide A pesticide used to kill molds and fungi.

herbicide A pesticide used to kill weeds and other plants.

insecticide A pesticide used to kill insects.

Integrated Pest Management (IPM) The use of a combination of strategies to control pests; often includes reduced use of chemical pesticides in combination with biological and physical controls, such as infecting insects with viruses and bacteria harmless to humans, and introducing sterile male insects to interrupt the reproductive cycle.

marine biomedicine The application of knowledge about organisms living in the sea to illness and its treatment.

microbiology The branch of biology that deals with microscopic life forms: viruses, bacteria, fungi, and protozoans.

molecular evolution The study of DNA and other genetic structures as they relate to the process by which life forms undergo change over time.

neurobiology The study of the development, structure, and function of the nervous system in various life forms.

oceanography The scientific study of the world's oceans and seas.

organochloride Chlorinated hydrocarbon. A class of synthetic chemicals made from hydrogen, carbon, and chlorine molecules; includes the highly toxic pesticides DDT, chlordane, aldrin, and dieldrin; banned for use in the United States.

organophosphate Alkyl or organic phosphate. A class of synthetic chemicals made from hydrogen, carbon, and phosphorus molecules; includes the highly toxic pesticides malathion and parathion; related to nerve gases.

pesticide Any agent used to kill pests, including insects, weeds, and fungi.

sensory physiology The study of the structure and function of the sense organs, including the brain and central nervous system, the skin, auditory, olfactory, and optic systems.

toxic, toxin Poisonous; a poison.

zoology The scientific study of the animal kingdom.

Further Reading

Baines, John. *Exploring Humans and the Environment.* Austin, TX: Raintree Steck-Vaughn, 1992.

Bernards, Neal, ed. *The Environmental Crisis: Opposing Viewpoints.* San Diego, CA: Greenhaven Press, 1991.

Billings, Charlene W. *Pesticides: Necessary Risk.* Springfield, NJ: Enslow, 1993.

Busch, Phyllis S. *Backyard Safaris: Fifty-two Year-Round Science Adventures.* New York: Simon & Schuster, 1995.

Carson, Rachel. *Edge of the Sea.* Boston: Houghton Mifflin, 1955.

———.*The Sea Around Us.* New York: Oxford University Press, 1961.

———. *The Sense of Wonder.* New York: Harper and Row, 1965.

———. *Silent Spring.* Boston: Houghton Mifflin, 1962.

———. *Under the Sea Wind.* 2d ed. New York: Truman Talley/Dutton, 1991.

Earth Works Project Staff. *Fifty Simple Things You Can Do to Save the Earth.* Pasadena, CA: Greenleaf, 1990.

Gay, Kathlyn. *Cleaning Nature Naturally.* New York: Walker & Co., 1991.

Grant, Lesley. *Great Careers for People Concerned About the Environment.* Detroit, MI: Gale Research, Inc., 1993.

Hare, Tony. *Polluting the Sea.* Danbury, CT: Franklin Watts, 1991.

Henricksson, John. *Rachel Carson: The Environmental Movement.* Brookfield, CT: Millbrook Press, 1991.

Hirschi, Ron. *Save Our Oceans and Coasts.* New York: Bantam, 1993.

Landau, Elaine. *Environmental Groups: The Earth Savers.* Springfield, NJ: Enslow, 1993.

Lawlor, Elizabeth P. *Discover Nature at the Seashore: Things to Know and Things to Do.* Mechanicsburg, PA: Stackpole, 1992.

Lee, Sally. *Pesticides.* Danbury, CT: Franklin Watts, 1991.

Maynard, Thane. *Saving Endangered Birds: Ensuring a Future in the Wild.* Danbury, CT: Franklin Watts, 1993.

Peacock, Graham and Hudson, Terry. *Exploring Habitats.* Austin, TX: Raintree Steck-Vaughn, 1992.

Reef, Catherine. *Rachel Carson: The Wonder of Nature.* New York: Twenty-First Century Books, 1992.

Wadsworth, Ginger. *Rachel Carson: Voice for the Earth.* Minneapolis, MN: Lerner, 1991.

Yount, Lisa. *Pesticides.* San Diego, CA: Lucent Books, 1994.

Zeff, Robin L. *Environmental Action Groups.* New York: Chelsea House, 1993.

SOURCES

"Analysis of Tree Bark Shows Global Spread of Insecticides." *New York Times*, October 10, 1995.

Brooks, Paul. *The House of Life: Rachel Carson at Work.* Boston: Houghton Mifflin Company, 1972.

Carson, Rachel. *Silent Spring.* Boston: Houghton Mifflin, 1962.

Carter, Jimmy. Public Papers of the Presidents of the United States, June 9, 1990.

Conservation Bulletin No. 33: *Food from the Sea: Fish and Shellfish of New England.* U.S. Government Printing Office, 1943.

Freeman, Martha, ed. *Always, Rachel.* Boston: Beacon Press, 1995.

Letter from Rachel Carson to the editor, *Reader's Digest*, August 1953.

"The Gentle Storm Center," *Life*, October 12, 1962, p. 105.

Hines, Bob. "Remembering Rachel." *Yankee*, June 1991, p. 64.

Index

Boldfaced, italicized page numbers include picture references.

Photo Credits

Cover (background): Photodisk; cover (inset) and pages 27, 29, 58, 77, 82, 87, 91, 99: AP/Wide World Photos; page 4: ©Bob Hines/reprinted by permission of the Rachel Carson History Project; pages 8, 9, 10, 13: Carson family photograph/reprinted by permission of the Rachel Carson History Project; page 15: Photo courtesy of Chatham College Archives; pages 16, 24: Reprinted by permission of the Rachel Carson History Project; page 21: ©George Whiteley/Photo Researchers, Inc.; page 22: ©Mary Frye/reprinted by permission of the Rachel Carson History Project; page 30: ©Dan Guravich/Photo Researchers, Inc.; page 32: ©Buddy Jenssen/Leo de Wys, Inc.; page 37: ©D. P. Wilson/Science Source/Photo Researchers, Inc.; page 40: ©Andrew J. Martinez/Photo Researchers, Inc.; page 45: ©Rod Planck/Photo Researchers, Inc.; page 47: ©Rachel Carson/reprinted by permission of the Rachel Carson History Project; pages 48, 69: ©North Wind Pictures; page 50: ©Douglas Faulkner/Photo Researchers, Inc.; pages 53, 71: ©Shirley A. Briggs/reprinted by permission of the Rachel Carson History Project; page 61: ©Lida Moser/reprinted by permission of the Rachel Carson History Project; page 64: ©Brooks Studio/reprinted by permission of the Rachel Carson History Project; page 66: ©Henryk Kaiser/Leo de Wys, Inc.; page 87: Courtesy John F. Kennedy Library; page 94: ©Martin Bond/Science Photo Library/Photo Researchers, Inc.; page 97: ©Holt Studios International/Nigel Cattlin/Photo Researchers, Inc.; page 104: Courtesy Jimmy Carter Library; page 105: ©Richard Glassman/Blackbirch Press, Inc. Artwork by Blackbirch Graphics, Inc.